6/25

Konstantin Paustovsky (1892-1968), was
one of the most popular writers in the
Soviet Union during his lifetime. Though
far from being an official apologist or
propagandist, in these stories Paustovsky
celebrates the beauty and goodness of his
country, in which he took a genuine pride.

RAINY DAWN

AND OTHER STORIES

KONSTANTIN PAUSTOVSKY

TRANSLATED AND WITH AN INTRODUCTION BY
DAVID AND **LYUDMILA MATTHEWS**

QUARTET BOOKS

First published in English by Quartet Books Limited 1995
A member of the Namara Group
27 Goodge Street, London W1P 2LD

Translation and Introduction copyright © by
David and Lyudmila Matthews 1995

A catalogue record for this title is available from the
British Library

ISBN 07043 0239X

Printed and bound by BPC Paperbacks Ltd

Contents

A Note on Russian Names

1   Russian names usually consist of three elements: *imya* (given name), *otchestvo* (patronymic), and *familiya* (surname). Thus Chekhov's full name was Anton Pavlovich Chekhov – Anton, son of Pavel Chekhov; Tchaikhovsky was Pyotr Ilyich Tchaikhovsky – Pyotr, son of Ilya Tchaikhovsky. The male patronymic often ends in the suffixes *–ich* or *–ovich*. Female patronymics often have the endings *–ovna* or *–yevna*, and female surnames, of which the masculine form ends in *–ov*, usually take the ending *–ova*. Thus Maria Pavlovna Chekhova – Maria, daughter of Pavel Chekhov; Olga Andreyevna Bashilova – Olga, daughter of Andrei, wife of Bashilov.

2   People are politely addressed or referred to by their given name and patronymic. This applies to Soviet, pre-Soviet and post-Soviet times: *Sergei Petrovich was an artist*; *'You must be Olga Andreyevna'*.

3   In fictional narrative it is customary to use just the surname for male characters: *Kuzmin sat down*; *Bashilov was in hospital*. Female characters are more usually referred to by the given name and the patronymic: *Nina Porfiryevna was a librarian*; *Maria Pavlovna was sitting in the garden*. Younger people and others referred to less formally are often introduced by the given name or its diminutive only: *Anfisa liked reading*; *Masha was a student*; *Timofei was a cabman*.

4   Most given names have one or several diminutives or familiar forms, which frequently alternate with the standard form. Thus Vladimir may also be referred to as Volodya, Vova or Vovka; Olga as Olya or Olenka. Such variants may be used for the same person in the space of one paragraph. The following diminutives occur in these stories (the standard forms are given in brackets):

male		female	
Alyosha	(Alexei)	Fenya	(Feodosiya)
Fedya	(Fyodr)	Katyusha	(Ekaterina)
Filka	(Filip)	Marfusha	(Marfa)
Kostya	(Konstantin)	Masha	(Maria)
Misha	(Mikhail)	Nastya	(Anastasia)
Pasha	(Pavel)	Natasha	(Natalya)
Sasha	(Aleksandr)	Olya	(Olga)
Styopa	(Stepan)	Sasha	(Aleksandra)
Vaska	(Vasily)	Varyusha	(Varvara)
Vitya	(Viktor)	Zhenya	(Yevgenia)
Zhora	(Georgy)		

Translators' Introduction

If one were called upon to single out one overriding characteristic shared by the people of the Soviet Union in the decades which followed the Second World War, this characteristic would undoubtedly be the great feeling of pride that most people had in the Motherland, in the vastness of its territory, in the goodness of its inhabitants and in its visible achievements.

This sense of national pride was of course engendered in children from their first day at school, where the curriculum emphasized all that was great and pure. Soviet literature, drama, art and cinema stressed the positive elements of life and its progress, and when they looked around them, people had little reason to disagree with the message they were given.

Such pride would manifest itself in the magnificence of annual events like the May Day Parade in Moscow, in the permanent exhibitions of national achievement to be found in every large city, in the once-in-a-lifetime visit to the Mausoleum of Vladimir Ilich Lenin in Red Square, where people from over the whole of the Soviet Union would queue for hours in any weather in order to file reverently past the embalmed body of the founder of their state, the leader to whom they owed much of what they had in their present life. Veterans who had witnessed the October Revolution, who had struggled in the Civil War and who had defended their country in what came to be known as The Great Patriotic War, were accorded due respect by the younger generation, and their accounts were listened to avidly by those who loved to share their experiences in that momentous period of history.

It was a matter of great pride to the average Soviet citizen that his country was the biggest in the world, stretching from the Baltic in the west to the Pacific in the east, that its land-mass contained such a vast and varied population, speaking innumerable tongues in remote areas, all living in harmony and striving to realize the now attainable socialist ideal.

By many, and perhaps by most, this sense of pride was genuinely felt, and often freely expressed to foreign visitors by Soviet colleagues and friends. It is, therefore, no cause for surprise that Konstantin Paustovsky (1892–1968), whose works give expression to this sentiment, was during his lifetime one of the most popular and most widely read writers in the Soviet Union. He more than most had the talent and skill to express in unforgettable words the feelings that so many of his fellow-countrymen experienced themselves about their own land and culture. His finely drawn descriptions of the natural beauty of the country were immediately recognizable to those who had travelled its vast distances; his tales of the war and its consequences were familiar to those who had themselves participated; his accounts of the simple goodness of people and their willingness to help others in times of difficulty made one feel good oneself; and finally his sometimes undisguised emotional romanticism, something in which Russians love to indulge themselves, could tug a string in every heart.

Konstantin Paustovsky was born in Moscow in 1892. His father worked as a railway station-master. He was an easy-going man, who loved to wander from place to place. His mother on the other hand was a strict disciplinarian who did not share the views of her husband. The result was that the family broke up, and the young Konstantin was obliged to find his own way in life.

Paustovsky began his education in a Kiev *gymnasium*, and in his youth wandered around the woods near the city, 'composing verse without restraint'. His early love for poetry never left him, and certainly manifests itself in the poetic quality of his prose. While still at school, he tells us, he wrote his first story, and there conceived the ambition of one day becoming a writer. After school, he entered the Natural History Faculty of Kiev University, and among other things seems to have acquired a firm scientific grounding in botany. This interest never left him. His almost encyclopaedic knowledge of flowers and plants is amply demonstrated in his writing, and his meticulous descriptions, such as that of the water-meadow in 'The Dog-Rose', cause translators of his stories no small problem.

Paustovsky completed his education at the Law Faculty of Moscow University in 1914. During the First World War he did not enter the army but, after working for a short time as a tram-driver, became a medical orderly on a hospital train. Therefore, he had the opportunity to travel widely in the very heart of Russia, whose woods and rivers he came to know and love. His work as a journalist for a Moscow newspaper, which he joined during the February Revolution of 1917, gave him the valuable experience essential for an aspiring writer. Assignments to Kiev and Odessa enabled him to meet and talk with many of those who had already established their reputation in letters, such as Ilf, Babel and Slavin. Journalism occupied his life in the 1920s and early 1930s, when he himself began to turn his attention to serious, progressive fiction. His first successful novels, *Kara-Bugaz* and *Kholkhida*, were inspired by what he observed of life by the Caspian and the Black Sea. He now turned away from the romanticism evoked by fictitious, exotic foreign lands, so much a part of the works of Aleksandr Grin, whom he greatly admired (but about whose novels he expressed delicate reservation in the brief sketches he wrote concerning his life), and began to look for his own heroes in the everyday situations which he had witnessed himself. The builders of dams and man-made seas, the sailors of the Volga, the lady librarian in a small, unknown town, the elderly horticulturalist, whose daughter disappoints him by yearning to go to drama school, the self-sacrificing spinster, Fenya, whose deeds of kindness might have forever remained unrecorded, and above all the soldiers and sailors, who in fact did nothing more remarkable than anyone else during their campaigns – these became Paustovsky's heroes, with whom everyone could identify and whom everyone had known in their own lifetime.

Typical in his view of Soviet life and society, Paustovsky was highly conscious of the value placed upon professional expertise. He was a writer and this was his profession, which should be carried out with as much care and seriousness as another skilled person might exercise in driving a train, navigating a boat, painting a picture, or directing a collective farm. In his view everything required equal talent, which needed to be developed in the direction of fulfilling a professional aim. Everything has its own beauty. In his story, 'The Run of Time', a famous artist, who probably thinks a little too highly of his calling, is put out when the girl-navigator refuses to stop her steamer so that he might complete his drawing. When he complains, he is quickly put in his place by the girl, who reminds him of the importance of observing a timetable. 'Ah, you people!' he says haughtily. 'You're like machines. You have no sense of life's beauty.' The girl is justifiably angry and asks him whether he finds no beauty in a professionally constructed network of transport designed to make life run smoothly for people like him. He cannot help but agree with her. When she finally sees his newly completed canvas on show in the Tretyakov Gallery, she in turn is amazed by the power of the artist, who found colours and vistas such as she had never seen herself on the river she had been navigating for the whole of her working life.

Paustovsky is always prepared to give due acknowledgement to the skill and perception of others, however simple or naïve these people might at first appear. While spending his summer on the outskirts of Voronezh, he learnt as much from the unschooled, little 'herdsman' about the native vegetation of the region as the boy learnt from his fascinating accounts of the theory of cross-pollination, and, as can be seen from the story, he also learnt a salutory lesson in life!

Although Paustovsky took his subjects from among such undistinguished and ordinary people, and set his stories in the life we see around us, like many Russian writers of his generation he found himself unable to escape from the unashamedly romantic side of the soul. The wonderment expressed by Aleksandr Grin, the popular appeal of the music of Tchaikovsky, Mozart and Grieg, the chance meeting of a man and a woman, which becomes love at first sight, are never far from his mind. Such overt, almost self-indulgent romanticism is to be found in stories like 'The Old Cook', 'The Basket of Fir-Cones' and 'Rainy Dawn'. We know that Mozart never met an old, blind cook and eased his dying with his youthful playing; Grieg's meeting with little Dagni, for whose eighteenth birthday the composer is imagined to have written one of his most exquisite pieces, never actually happened; could the soldier, Kuzmin, really have fallen so quickly in love with his friend's wife to whom he was merely delivering a letter from the Front? But does that matter? Paustovsky's beautiful, quiet descriptions are enough to convince us for a moment that these illusions must be true.

Paustovsky expresses his conviction in the following words: 'A tale is necessary not only for children but also for grown-ups. It brings out our agitation – the source of mighty human passions. It does not allow us to relax, but always shows us sparkling new horizons, another life. It is demanding and makes us yearn passionately for such a life.'

Again in a well-established Russian tradition, Paustovsky also wrote many stories for children, often, according to Soviet taste, pointing a definite, uplifting moral. The story, 'Hot Bread', in which a surly boy ill-treats a lame horse, thereby bringing shame upon himself and disaster on his village, contains a theme frequently found in the literature on which Soviet children were brought up. The moral is simply that no one can be excused a misdeed without making suitable and sincere amends.

In his writings, Konstantin Paustovsky, though far from being an official apologist or propagandist, celebrates the beauty and goodness of his country, which he closely observed, loved and in which he took a genuine pride.

The Breeze

The whole day it had been raining with a cold, blustery wind. You often have this sort of weather in Moscow at the beginning of May. Everything was grey: the sky, the smoke hanging over the roofs, even the air. Only the asphalt glistened, like a black river.

A young naval officer came to visit an elderly doctor, a bachelor, who lived in a tall block of flats on the banks of the Moscow River. The sailor had been badly wounded in 1942 during the Siege of Sevastopol and had been sent behind the lines. The doctor attended to him for a long time and finally they became friends. Now the sailor had come on a few days' leave from the Black Sea Fleet. The doctor invited him to his home for a bottle of Kakhetian,[1] and invited him to stay overnight.

It was midnight when the radio announced the capture of Sevastopol by our troops. The firework display was timed for one o'clock in the morning – a time when the streets of Moscow are usually completely deserted. As they waited for it to start, the doctor and the sailor chatted together in the dimly lit office.

'It's curious,' said the doctor, finishing the last of the wine, 'what people think about when they are seriously wounded. For instance, what were you thinking about when you were in Sevastopol?'

'More than anything, I was afraid I might lose my packet of Kazbek cigarettes,' answered the sailor. 'I'm sure you know that on the label there's a picture of Mount Kazbek covered with snow. I was wounded at dawn. It was still fresh after the night. An early sun was shining through the haze – the start of a sultry, oppressive day. I was losing a lot of blood but kept on thinking about that packet and about the snow on Mount Kazbek. I wanted to be buried in the snow. I was sure that it would stop the flow of blood and make it easier for me to breathe. All the time the sun was rising. I was lying in the shadow of a ruined fence, and with every passing minute the shade grew less and less. Finally the sun began to burn my feet and then my arm. It took me a long time to raise my hand and alter its position in order to shade my eyes with my palm. I still couldn't feel any particular pain, but I remember quite clearly that all the time I kept worrying about that packet of cigarettes.'

'Why were you so afraid you might lose it?'

'How can I explain? Almost all new arrivals at the front have a silly habit of writing the address of their next-of-kin on anything they drag around with them. On their gas-mask covers, on their map-cases, on the lining of their forage-caps. They're always afraid they'll be killed without leaving a trace. Later on, of course, it wears off.'

'Whose address had you written on your cigarette packet?' asked the doctor, cunningly screwing up his eyes.

The sailor flushed and gave no answer.

'Very well,' said the doctor, hurriedly passing over the subject. 'Let's leave that question.'

At that very moment, the doorbell of his flat rang. The doctor went into the hall and opened the door. The voice of a young woman, out of breath, sounded from the darkness.

'They're having a firework display. Can I watch from your balcony?'

'Well, of course you can,' answered the doctor. 'But what do you think you're doing, running up five flights of stairs like that? Do you want to ruin your heart? Turn the light out,' called the doctor to the sailor from the passageway, 'and we'll go out on to the balcony. Only put your overcoat on. It hasn't stopped raining yet.'

The sailor got up and turned off the light. He greeted the unknown woman in the hall. Their fingers collided in the darkness. The woman felt for the sailor's hand and shook it gently.

They went out on to the balcony. There was the smell of iron roofs and autumn. The early spring often resembles the autumn.

'So,' said the doctor, shivering in the rain, 'so what happened to your packet of Kazbeks?'

'When I came round, the packet of Kazbeks was missing. The hospital staff had probably thrown it away, or the nurse who dressed my wounds. But what I found strange . . .'

'Strange?'

'Yes. I mean the person whose name I had written on the packet received a letter saying that I had been wounded. I didn't write myself.'

'Nothing strange about that,' said the doctor. 'Someone took the packet, saw the address and wrote. The most usual thing to happen. It seems to me that you're trying to attach some exaggerated importance to the matter.'

'Not at all,' said the sailor, a little embarrassed. 'Anyway that letter about me at that time turned out to be unnecessary.'

'Why?'

'Well, you see,' hesitated the soldier. 'Love is like the breeze. In the day, it blows from the sea on to the shore, and at night, from the shore on to the sea. Not everyone waits for us as faithfully and as patiently as we should like.'

'You're talking like a real poet,' remarked the doctor with a smile.

'Good heavens!' exclaimed the woman. 'What a prosaic man you are, doctor!'

'No, please!' the doctor burst out indignantly.

At that moment, the first salvo erupted with its purple fire. The thunder of cannons resounded over the roofs. Hundreds of rockets flew up into the dull sky, hissing in the rain. The flames of the rockets were reflected in the asphalt, lighting the city and the Kremlin with a flood of colour. For a few brief moments, the city emerged from the darkness. The inhabitants of the tall block caught a glimpse of what they saw every day: the Kremlin, the wide bridges, the churches and flats of Zamoskvorechye[2] on the opposite bank of the river.

But everything looked quite different from how it looked in the light of day. The Kremlin seemed suspended in air, so light and delicate. The fleeting glow of the rockets and the rainy mist softened the harsh lines of its cathedrals, its fortress towers and the belfry of Ivan the Great. The majestic buildings lost their heaviness. They emerged like flashes of light in the powdery smoke of the fireworks. They seemed to be made of white stone, bathed on the outside in a rosy flame. When the string of fireworks went out, the buildings also lost their radiance, as if they had been the very source of this pulsating light.

'Just like fairyland,' said the woman. 'It's a pity the display only had twenty-four rounds in it and not a hundred and twenty-four.' She fell silent, then added: 'Sevastopol! Do you remember how green the water is there? Especially under the stern of the ferries. And the scent of the dry acacias, smashed by the explosions?'

'What do you mean "remember"?' said the doctor. 'Whom are you asking? I've never been to Sevastopol.'

The woman gave no answer.

'I remember it all very well,' said the sailor. 'Have you been to Sevastopol?'

'I was there roughly at the same time as you,' answered the woman.

The display had finished. The woman left, but returned in a few minutes, complaining of a headache. She asked the doctor for some tablets and then left again, with embarrassed apologies.

During the night, the sailor woke up and looked out of the window. The rain had stopped; stars were shining in the gaps between the clouds. 'The weather's changing,' thought the sailor. 'That's why I can't sleep.' He dozed off again, but a drawling voice right next to him said: 'How transparent the water is there!' He awoke, opened his eyes and looked around, but of course there was no one in the room.

He stretched out his arm towards the packet of cigarettes lying on the chair, but it was empty. He remembered that he had another in his overcoat pocket. The sailor got up, put on his dressing-gown, which was hanging over the back of the chair, went out into the passage and switched on the light. On a little table by the mirror, on top of his naval cap, lay a torn, crumpled packet of Kazbeks. A large, black stain covered the drawing of the snowy mountains.

Still without understanding, the sailor took the packet and opened it. There was nothing inside. But on the reverse of the flap he saw the familiar address, written in his own handwriting. 'How did that come here?' he thought. 'Surely not . . .' A little shaken, he quickly turned off the light and, squeezing the packet in his hand, returned to his room. He lay awake till dawn.

The next morning, he said nothing to the doctor. He

took a long time to shave, then bathed in cold water. His hands were trembling. 'Stupid!' thought the sailor. 'What the hell!'

A mist suffused with sunlight lay over Moscow. The windows were open wide, and the freshness from the night poured into them. The morning came up in the damp gleam of the rain which had stopped a little while before, and heralded a long summer with warm showers, limpid sunsets, lime-tree blossoms under the feet.

The sailor was convinced that this morning could not have been any different. The quietness of the dawn, so rare in Moscow, did not quell his anxiety but strengthened it. 'To hell with it!' he said softly. 'After all such things do happen in life.'

He guessed that the woman had worked, obviously as a nurse, in Sevastopol. She had been the first to dress his wounds, had found the cigarette packet with the address and had written the letter to the person – the other woman – who had forgotten him so easily and so quickly. The evening before, she had heard his story, recognized him and then on purpose had brought out this packet of Kazbeks.

But why had she kept it? Why had she not said anything? 'Because she's young,' he decided. 'I like mysteries like that as well. But I'll have to call on her to thank her.' Then he realized what extraordinary courage he would need to ring her doorbell, and could scarcely make up his mind to do it.

Within the hour, the sailor had walked out of the doctor's flat. He descended the stairs very slowly, and stopped on the third floor. Three doors gave on to the landing. With a feeling of relief he remembered that he had not asked the doctor in which flat the woman lived or what her name was. It was an awkward question. And now he could hardly go round ringing all the bells asking for a total stranger.

At that moment, from behind one of the doors, the sailor heard a familiar voice. 'I'll be back in an hour, Masha. I didn't sleep well last night. It's so close in here. I'll take a walk down to the river.'

The sailor realized that now, at that very minute, she would come out and find him on the landing. He rushed to the door and with his heart pounding rang the bell.

The door opened at once, and there stood the woman he had met the evening before. The wind blew through the flat and out of the door, ruffling her light dress and her hair.

The sailor said nothing. The woman came out, closed the door behind her, took him by the hand and said, 'Come on. I'll accompany you.'

'I wanted to thank you,' said the sailor. 'You saved my life there in Sevastopol. And you sent a letter to that address . . .'

'It seems that my letter didn't have much success,' said the woman with a smile. 'You're not angry with me, are you?'

They went down the staircase. She let go of his hand and brushed her hair back.

'Why should I be angry?' asked the sailor. 'It's all very strange. And good . . .'

The woman stopped and looked into his eyes. 'You shouldn't worry. I worry myself as much as you.'

They went down on to the embankment and stopped by the iron railings. The pink walls of the Kremlin shimmered through the morning mist. The woman shaded her eyes with her hand and stood silently. As he looked at her hand, the sailor thought that his own blood must have been on those fingers. On those delicate, dear fingers.

Without removing her hand from her eyes, the woman said, 'I never believed that it could be like this . . . so suddenly. And that I would ever see you again after Sevastopol.'

The sailor took her arm. He kissed her small, strong hand, paying no attention to the passers-by, who walked on as if they had noticed nothing. It was only when they had gone a respectable distance that they stole a glance and smiled with embarrassment.

1944

The Birth of a Story

Early hours in the winter; the suburban Moscow day was still drowsy; quite impossible to wake up after the long, drawn-out night. Lamps were burning here and there in the cottages; snow fell intermittently.

The author Muravyov emerged into the corridor of the train, opened the outer door and for a long time gazed at the winter passing alongside the carriage.

It was no longer the depths of winter, but 'the little winter', as they call the last days of the cold, when the sky is overcast, when the damp wind rushes by you in gusts, and suddenly the thaw sets in, and the first drops of melting snow fly from the branches. In such a season, springs cautiously begin to stir under the ice in forest ravines, and with the water they bring a host of air-bubbles. Hastily the bubbles speed in silver rows, some sticking to the limp underwater weeds. And some grey bullfinch with a pink breast sits squarely on a branch over the spring, and with one eye he looks at the bubbles rushing up, makes a sudden cheep and shakes the snow from his feathers. It will soon be the end of winter.

There are days when life seems to us particularly clear and harmonious. At that moment, Muravyov experienced such a feeling.

In an earlier age, writers loved to address themselves

to their readers with all manner of questions. 'Why,' thought Muravyov, 'shouldn't modern authors sometimes make use of this old, well-tried device? Why, for instance, shouldn't I start a story in this way:

Have you ever experienced, my esteemed reader, that feeling of inescapable joy which suddenly takes over the whole of your being without any recognizable cause? You are walking along a street and all of a sudden something extraordinary has happened on the earth. Have you ever felt this way? Certainly, you have. Have you ever sought the cause of that feeling? I doubt it. But even if the premonition of happiness eluded you, it contained in itself the force that enabled you to go on living.

To seek out and discover the causes of the obscure but still fruitful human condition is the business of writers,' thought Muravyov. 'It is still one of the provinces of our labour.'

Labour! At this moment, everything around him was full of it. Goods-trains weighing a thousand tons trundled towards him with the hiss of steam and crash of pistons. That was labour. An aeroplane flew low, humming over the snowy fields. That was also labour. The steel masts of the electric transmitters, white with hoar-frost, carried their powerful current through the dark. Even that was labour.

'For what reason does our vast country of countless millions, now covered with snow, work?' thought Muravyov. 'And, after all, why do I work? For life? For high spiritual values? For the reason that mankind might be perfect, honest and intelligent? So that finally love might fill our days with its clean, pure breath? Yes, for that.

'In his lyrical verses, Pushkin asked: "Who tended the pure roses of Theocritus amid the snows? In this age of iron, who guessed at gold?" Indeed, we are the ones,' Muravyov himself answered the question.

The snow flew by the open door of the carriage and melted on his face. 'Who else but us?'

Muravyov was writing a story about 'labour' for a Moscow journal. He had been working at the story for hours but nothing had come of it. Perhaps it was because his detailed account of labour excluded the human element, and without human beings the story had become unbearably tedious. It seemed to Muravyov that his story was suffering from the turmoil of life in Moscow – the telephone calls, the scores of business affairs, the obligation to receive guests and visit friends. Finally, Muravyov came to the end of his tether and took leave of the city. A friend of his had a *dacha*[3] in one of those villages outside Moscow. He decided to move in and stay there until he had finished the story. The house was inhabited by some distant relations of his friend, but Muravyov had never met them.

In the Sevyerny Station, as Muravyov was walking along the platform to the suburban train, he suddenly felt a deep pounding in his heart and sensed that his work would turn out successfully. Now he was convinced that, without a doubt, he would achieve something. He knew it from many clear signs, from the freshness that pervaded his whole body, from his restrained anxiety, that particular awareness with which he now took notice and remembered everything around him, from his impatient desire to reach the unknown cottage as soon as possible, so that he might sit quietly at the table with a thick heap of blank paper before him; indeed he knew it from the fact that the whole time fragments of his favourite verses came to his memory: 'My soul is constrained by lyric emotion; it shudders and resounds and seeks, as if in a dream, to gush out at last in manifest freedom.'[4]

In the same state of anxious elation, Muravyov got

down from the train on to the long country platform amid the pine forests. The platform was deserted. Only the sparrows sat on the railings, their feathers sticking up, eyeing the train with displeasure. They did not even hop aside when Muravyov walked by them, almost brushing them with his sleeve. Just one of the sparrows chirped peevishly after him. 'He's probably angry with me for being such an ignoramus,' thought Muravyov, glancing back at the sparrow. 'Just think on, my lord!' he said. The sparrow kept his suspicious, beady eyes on him for a long time until he was out of sight.

The cottage was three kilometres from the station. Muravyov walked along the deserted road. Sometimes the fields were visible among the copses. The sky above them was pink.

'It can't be sunset already,' said Muravyov loudly, and suddenly became aware of the fact that here outside the city he had begun to talk to himself.

The day was fading quickly and almost without benefit of light. Not even one sunbeam pierced the thick gloom, nor fell upon the frosty branches, chasing over them with pale fire or throwing tenuous shadows on to the snow. The road followed the ravine down to the log-bridge. Underneath, a stream murmured.

'Aha!' cried Muravyov with a joy beyond understanding, and stopped. The dark running water was visible through the ice in a small gully, and below it the rocky depths. 'Where do you find so much water from in the winter, my friend?' asked Muravyov.

The stream, of course, gave no answer. It continued to murmur, now quietly, now raising its voice to a peal. The water broke the limpid blocks of ice and sent them crashing against each other. Muravyov made his way down to the stream and began to hit the pieces of ice with his stick. The water of the stream foamed around the broken ice.

'Anyway, the spring needs a little help,' he thought,

laughing at himself. He glanced around. On the bridge
stood a girl wearing a blue ski-suit and, with her sticks
firmly placed in the snow, she was looking intently at
Muravyov.

He was embarrassed. What on earth must that girl be
thinking of him? 'Silly old fool acting like a child!' Of
course, she couldn't think anything else. But the girl
bent down, detached her skis and cried to Muravyov,
'Hang on! You'd do better to break the ice with my ski-
sticks. They've got iron tips.'

She ran down to the stream and held out her stick to
him. As it happened, it *was* easier to smash the ice
with that. They both set about breaking the ice in silent
concentration. Muravyov felt hot and took off his mittens. The girl's hair started to fall down from beneath
her knitted woollen hat.

Then a little boy wearing a cap with ear-flaps sticking
out in opposite directions appeared as if from nowhere.
Muravyov noticed him when he knocked against him
in the excitement, sniffing and getting in the way.

'I've had enough,' said Muravyov at last, straightening
himself. The dense twilight gloom already lay over the
earth. 'How quickly the time has passed,' thought
Muravyov. He glanced at the girl and burst out laughing.
The girl shook the snow from her mittens and in answer
to him smiled without raising her eyes.

As they made their way up from the ravine to the
forest path, Muravyov chatted with the girl. The boy
trudged behind them for a while, sniffing and breathing
heavily through his nose.

It turned out that the girl was living with her father
in the *dacha* to which Muravyov himself was heading.

'So that means you must be a distant relation of my
friend,' said Muravyov with great pleasure, and introduced himself. The girl took off her wet mitten and
held out her hand.

'My name is Zhenya,' she said without ceremony.

'Papa and I have been expecting you for two days. I shan't get in your way. No, really, you mustn't think ... It's the last day of my holidays tomorrow. I'm going back to the Institute in Moscow. But my papa ...'

'What about your papa?' asked Muravyov, pricking up his ears.

'He's a botanist – and he's very talkative,' answered Zhenya. 'But yesterday, he gave me his word of honour that he wouldn't wear you out with his talk. Only I don't know whether he'll keep his promise. He finds it difficult to control himself.'

'How do you mean?' asked Muravyov.

Zhenya walked along by his side. She was carrying her skis over her shoulder and looking straight ahead. The faint light shone into her eyes and on to the broad polished blades of the skis with the turned-up ends. Muravyov was surprised and wondered where the light was coming from. The dark gloom had already settled over the surrounding fields for the night. Then he noticed that it was not, as he had first thought, the gleam of the snow, but the reflection of the broad illuminated window of the large two-storeyed *dacha*, which they were approaching.

'Well, why should it be so difficult to refrain from conversation?' asked Muravyov once more.

'How can I explain ...?' Zhenya hesitated. 'I know, for example, how a ship is built, or how fine linen is produced by the fingers of a weaver. But how books are written, that I can't understand. And neither can Papa.'

'Aha!' drawled Muravyov. 'You won't talk about that in passing.'

'But won't you be writing about it?' Zhenya asked diffidently, and Muravyov realized that if she had not been so shy, she would have asked him to write on the subject. Of course, other people write about their own work.

Muravyov stopped, and screwing up his eyes gazed

fixedly at Zhenya. Suddenly he smiled. 'Well done! How did you guess what I'm writing . . .? I mean, that's just what I am thinking of doing, writing about my own work as a writer.'

'I didn't even guess,' said Zhenya timidly. 'I just said it, that's all. But I should love to know how characters like Katyusha Maslova or Telegin in *The Road to Calvary*[5] are suddenly brought into the world and then live for centuries. That's why I asked.'

But Muravyov was not listening to what she was saying. His mind was made up; he would write about his own labour. Why had the idea not occurred to him before? How could he write, detached and without feeling, about what he did not know, about what he had not experienced? To write and feel tongue-tied, knowing that your words have ceased to evoke anger, tears, thought and laughter, but rattle like empty tin-cans – how ridiculous!

That very evening, without the slightest pang of regret, Muravyov threw into the stove, hot and crackling with dry birchwood, everything he had written during the last days in Moscow.

On the table lay a thick pile of blank paper. He sat down before the table and began to write on the first page:

An old botanist – a thin, restless man with rapid gestures – was telling me this evening of how plants behave under the snow, how the sprouts of the colts-foot slowly make their way through the icy crust, and how the cold flowers of the snowdrops open underneath the surface of the snow. He has promised to take me to the forest tomorrow, to remove with great care the upper layer of the snow in one of the glades and to let me see for myself these flowers of the winter which still lack colour.

I am attempting to write a story or a sketch – and

I am myself unable to name everything that flows from my pen – about a phenomenon, as yet unresearched by anyone, which bears the rather high-flown title of 'creative work'.

If we look at the best examples of prose, we see that they are full of genuine poetry and artistry.

Naïve people, some of them poets with their watery eyes full of colourless dreams, still think to this day that as the world becomes less mysterious, so the tedium of our existence increases. But this is nonsense. I am convinced that poetry is to a large extent born of awareness. The quantity of poetry grows in accordance with the quantity of our knowledge. The less mystery there is and the more powerful human reasoning becomes, the greater is the perception with which man is able to express to others the poetry of our earth.

An example of this is the old botanist's account of the life of plants in the winter. The most wonderful poem could be written on this subject. It should be composed in verse as cold and white as the flowers under the snow.

From the very start, I wish to establish the thought that the sources of poetry and prose consist of two things – knowledge and the power of human imagination. Knowledge is the tuber from which the unseen and eternal flowers of fancy grow. I beg your forgiveness for such a precious comparison, but I feel it is time to forget our 'highly cultured' prejudices which condemn elegance and many other things that are no less good. What matters is employing them in the right place and in proper measure.

Muravyov wrote without stopping. He feared to lay down his pen for a moment lest the flow of his thoughts and words might cease.

He wrote of his labour, of the strength and grandeur

of the Russian language, of its greatest masters; he described how the whole world in all its dazzling variety must be reproduced with complete faithfulness in the pages of books, but projected through the crystal of the writer's mind and imagination, somehow more clearly conceived than it is in jarring reality. He wrote as if possessed, urgently, hurriedly. Outside in the narrow band of light that emanated from his window, the flurrying snow flew obliquely through the pine trees. It emerged from the gloom and immediately disappeared into the same darkness.

'At this moment outside the windows, the snow is flying on the wind, [wrote Muravyov]. Crystals of frozen water speed by. We all know their complicated and magnificent patterns. The man who could have invented the shape of such crystals would have deserved the highest honour. But there is nothing so transitory as those crystals. To obliterate them it takes only the breath of a child.

Nature possesses unbounded generosity. It never stints its force. We, people in general and writers in particular, would benefit by taking a lesson from nature. Most of all from its generosity. To all that we create, be it even the most insignificant story, we must give our whole being, our whole strength without reserve, all that is the very best in us. Here there is no room for thrift and economy.

We must, in the terms of an engineer, open all the floodgates, and never fear that sense of exhaustion which comes unavoidably when the work is done. You should feel as if you cannot write another sentence, that you have been squeezed dry like a sponge. This is a false illusion. For within a week you will once more be drawn towards the paper. The whole world will once more be in turmoil before your mind's eye.

As the ocean wave brings to the shore a cockle-shell or an autumn leaf and then returns to the sea quietly rattling its pebbles, in the same way your consciousness brings out and deposits on the paper before you the first word of your new work.'

Muravyov wrote until morning. As he put down his last words, the sky outside the window was turning dark blue. Over the gloom of the fields in a frosty haze the dawn was breaking. Downstairs he could hear the roar of the fire which had just been lit, and the rattling of the cast-iron oven door in the draught.

Muravyov wrote his last lines:

'Gorky used to say that you should never write in a vacuum. While you are working, you should always keep in mind the kind of person to whom you are relating all the best that you have stored in your heart and soul. Then you will find fresh and powerful words. We shall ever be grateful to Gorky for this simple, yet important advice.'

In the morning, Muravyov took a long bath, pouring over himself buckets of cold water in which floated pieces of transparent ice. Outside the window of the small bathroom, the branch of the fir tree hung down, bent under the weight of the snow. The fresh, coarse towel smelt of the wind.

His mind was light and empty – the feeling permeated his whole body.

Later in the day, Muravyov accompanied Zhenya to the station. She was going to Moscow to join her institute.

'To tell you frankly,' Muravyov told Zhenya when they reached the wooden platform in the forest, 'I'm ready to go back to Moscow myself. But I'll stay here for a day or two and rest.'

'You mean you didn't enjoy your stay here with us?' Zhenya asked timidly.

'No, no, on the contrary. It's wonderful to be here with you. Only I almost finished my story last night.'

'Almost finished?' was the involuntary reaction. For some reason, he was ashamed to admit that he had written the whole thing in the space of just one night. He wanted to tell Zhenya that he rushed in order to be able to read her his story before her departure to Moscow, but had not brought himself to do so. He wanted to tell her that he had written the story thinking of her; that Gorky had been right, and he was just grateful to her – practically a stranger – because she was alive in the world, and evoked the need for him to relate to her the very best that he had stored in his soul.

But Muravyov said nothing to Zhenya. Taking his leave, he grasped her hand tightly, looked into her confused eyes and thanked her for her help.

'What do you mean – for my help?' said Zhenya in astonishment.

Before the arrival of the train, the snow came down with heavy flakes. In the distance beyond the signal, the locomotive whistled in prolonged exultation. Suddenly the train emerged from the snow, as if from a white, enchanted land, and with a screech of brakes stopped.

Zhenya was the last to mount the steps. She did not go straight into the carriage, but stood at the door, blushing and smiling, and as a token of farewell waved her hand to Muravyov – the hand in the familiar green mitten.

The train went off into the snow, enveloping the forest in steam. Muravyov stood on the platform looking at it, and he felt once more, as he had done on the Sevyerny Station in Moscow, a pounding in the depths of his heart. He was overcome once more by the sudden feeling that at that very moment, somewhere nearby, on the earth lying silent under a seemingly light burden of driving snow, something very good had happened, and that he, Muravyov, was part of it.

'Well!' said Muravyov. 'One should not live too far away from youth.'

He went down from the platform by the frosty stairway and walked to the stream to smash the ice. He had taken the ski-stick with him.

1954

The Dog-rose

By night, fog had descended over the river. The steamer could go no farther and neither buoys nor warning lights were visible through the gloom. The boat hugged the steep bank in a silence that was broken only by the even creaking of the gangplanks thrown over on to the shore. Along the planks the sailors had run out the tie-ropes and had fastened them around an old brittle-willow.

Masha Klimova woke up in the middle of the night. It was so quiet that she could hear a passenger snoring in the far cabin. She sat up in her berth. Through the open window came a fresh flow of air sweetened by the smell of the willow leaves. Bushes, indistinct in the fog, were overhanging the deck and it seemed to Masha that in some incredible way the steamer was on land in a grove of shrubs. Then she heard the soft lapping of the water and guessed that the boat was moored alongside the bank.

In the bushes something clicked and then became silent. Then came another click followed by silence, as if the one making the clicks was listening intently and testing the stillness and responsiveness of the night by the sound. Soon the clicking changed to a long trill and was interrupted by a short whistle. At once a score of birds' voices responded to the whistle, and a sudden song of nightingales echoed through the thicket.

'Hear that, Yegorov?' someone asked from above, probably on the captain's bridge.

'Never heard such a chorus of nightingales, even on the Sheksna,' a hoarse voice answered from below.

Masha smiled and stretched out her hands before her. They seemed very brown in the dim light of the night – only the nails of her fingers showed up white.

'Why should I feel so sad? I just don't know,' said Masha in a low voice. 'Am I waiting for something? But what I'm waiting for I don't know myself.' She remembered her grandmother saying that in the world there is no maiden's sadness that cannot be understood. 'Rubbish!' she said. 'What maiden's sadness? It's just that my life is beginning. That's why it's a bit terrifying.'

Masha had just finished at the Forestry Institute and was now on her way from Leningrad to the Lower Volga to work on a collective, planting forests. When she thought that this was only 'a *bit* terrifying', she was of course deceiving herself. It was *really* terrifying. She imagined how she would come to the forestry division, and the boss – inevitably a dusty, surly fellow in a black jacket with bulging pockets and wearing boots smothered in lumps of clay – would look at her, look at her grey eyes (eyes which she always thought of as tin saucers), at her plaits, and would think: 'Wonderful! Just what we needed! Another load of young girls with pigtails! Now she'll go on repeating what's written in her textbooks. But what's the good of that to us? When the dry Astrakhan wind gets started, my dear, your textbooks won't be much help to you here.'

Throughout the long journey, Masha had got used to the thought of a surly boss in a black jacket and had stopped fearing him. But her sadness had not departed. Masha probably did not know that this was not sadness but a feeling which as yet has no name, if you like, a sinking of the heart before an unknown future, before the simple beauty of nature with its rivers, mists, deep nights and the noise of white willows on the bank.

Sleep would not come. Masha got dressed and went out on deck. Everything was covered in dew – the railings, the wire netting along the side, and the wicker chairs. On the forecastle she heard a muffled conversation.

'So I say to him,' a young sailor was recounting, ' "Come on, grandad, give me a smoke!" So he gives me the end of his fag. I have a drag and ask him, "What are you doing here, grandad, at night, alone, in the meadows?" "I guard the dawn," he says, and laughs to himself. "This might be the last dawn of my existence. But you," he says, "can't understand that. You're a young fellow." '

The sailors fell silent. The clicking of the nightingales once more began in the bushes. Masha leant over the railing. Somewhere far off in the gloom cocks began to crow in unison. Over there in the fog there must be a village.

'Those cocks? Are they the first or the second...?' She thought for a while that she was unable to distinguish the first from the second. She had read about this scores of times in books, but still she did not know.

Her grandmother, the widow of a river-captain, had advised Masha to take the steamer. Masha was glad that she had obeyed her. The steamer had started to follow the dark blue Neva, then cut across the Ladoga. It was the first time that Masha had seen its grey water and stone lighthouses on the low-lying capes. She saw the turbulent Svir, the sluices of the Maryinsky canal, its banks overgrown with horse-tail, and unknown boys on the jetties fishing with concentration for bleaks with their crooked rods.

The passengers changed but she found them all interesting. At Byelozyorsk, they were joined by an aircraft pilot, still young but with greying temples. He had probably been on leave at Byelozyorsk at his mother's, a frail old lady who wore a grey calico dress. She had been quietly sobbing on the jetty as she saw her son off, and the pilot was calling out to her from the deck: 'Don't forget, mother. That fish I caught, I've hung it in the cellar behind the stairs. Give one of the perches to Vaska.'

'I shan't forget, Pasha, I shan't forget at all,' nodded the old lady, drying her tears with a handkerchief rolled up into a ball.

The pilot smiled, joked and waved without taking his eyes off her, but his cheeks were twitching.

The steamer was boarded by actors. They made a lot of noise, cracked jokes, immediately introduced themselves to all the passengers. Now in the saloon, the piano damp from the river mists never stopped playing. An elderly actor, quick with a stern face, sang more than the others. Masha was surprised by his songs – she had never heard any of them before. Most frequently, the actor would sing a Polish song about a thief who was in love. The thief never managed to steal a star from the night sky for his beloved, and for this reason the young girl chased him away. Every time the actor finished this song, he noisily banged down the lid of the piano and said: 'The moral of this song is clear! Be condescending to someone in love. Don't object! That's the end of the conversation!' He would then straighten the bow of his black tie, sit himself down at the table and order some beer and a roach for himself.

At Cherepovets a few students from an architectural institute turned up on the steamer. They were returning to Moscow from the Kirillo-Byelozyorsky monastery. They had gone to the monastery for practice – to make measurements and sketches of the old buildings. Throughout the whole journey, the students argued about the stone carvings, the vaults, Andrei Rublyov and the high-rise buildings in Moscow. Masha, when she heard them, only blushed out of her own ignorance.

When the students joined the boat, the middle-aged actor went sort of quiet and stopped singing his little song about the thief. He spent the whole of his time sitting on deck reading Stanislavsky's *My Life and Art*. When he read, he wore glasses, which made him look more kindly and older. It became clear to Masha that all those pompous thespian tirades were just an inveterate habit, and that the man was much better than he wanted to appear.

Now all the passengers were sleeping – the pilot, the actors and the students. Only Masha stood on the deck listening to the sounds of the night, trying to guess what they were. Far away there was a rumble in the sky, which slowly became silent – probably an aircraft flying above the fog. Below the bank a fish splashed, and then in the distance was the sound of a shepherd's horn. It sang out so far away that at first Masha was unable to make out the real nature of those protracted, sweet sounds.

Someone struck a match behind Masha's back. She turned round and there stood the pilot smoking a *papirosa*. He threw the burning match into the water. It fell slowly through the mist and a whispy rainbow surrounded its flame.

'The nightingales won't let me sleep,' said the pilot, and although Masha could not see, she guessed that he was smiling in the darkness. Just like the words of a song:

Nightingales,[6] nightingales! Don't disturb the soldiers!
Let the soldiers sleep for a while.

'I've never known nightingales like this,' said Masha. 'Travel the length and breadth of the Soviet Union, and you'll know a lot more than that,' answered the pilot. 'Such a country you'd never see in your wildest dreams.'

'That's because you fly,' remarked Masha. 'And the earth changes all the time under your wings.'

'I don't think so,' he answered and fell silent for a while. 'It's getting light,' he said at last. 'There's blue in the east ... Where are you going?'

'To Kamyshin.'

'Yes, there's a small town called that on the Volga. Hot weather, watermelons, tomatoes ...'

'And you?'

'Me? Farther on.'

The pilot leant over the rail and watched the dawn turning to fire. The shepherd's horn sang even closer, the wind picked up and the fog began to lift. It drifted in chunks over the river. The wet bushes came slowly into view and amongst them a cabin, woven from willows. Near the cabin a fire was sending up smoke.

Masha was also looking at the dawn. On the edge of the sky, which was turning to gold, the last star was burning up like a drop of silver water.

'From today,' she thought, 'I shall be living in quite a different way. Before, I never used to notice things as I should, but now I'll take notice of everything. I'll remember things and store them in my heart.'

The pilot glanced at Masha. 'The girl's lost in her thoughts,' he muttered, turning his head away. Then he looked at her again and recalled the words of a novel he had read a long time ago: *There is nothing more wonderful in the world than the eyes of children and the eyes of young girls in the morning. The night is still dark in them, but even so they reflect the sparkle of the dawn.* 'Quite well put, really. Not so stupid,' thought the pilot.

The weather-beaten captain's mate, wearing his canvas mac, ran down from the bridge. 'Not sleeping?'

he called out chirpily to Masha. 'We've got an hour before we weigh anchor. You can go and have a stroll on shore if you like.'

'Yes. I might go,' Masha said to the pilot. 'I'll have time to cut some flowers.'

'Why not?' agreed the pilot. 'Come on. Let's go.'

They went down the shaky gangplank to the shore. An old man climbed out of the cabin, probably the same one who had been guarding the dawn during the night. At that moment the sun emerged from the mist. The grasses bunched around them, dark green like the murky, deep water. They were still exhaling the sharp cold of the night.

'What do you do for a living, grandad?' the pilot asked the old man.

'I'm a basket weaver,' answered the old fellow with a guilty smile. 'I weave a bit. Fishing-net frames, baskets for potatoes on the farm, make sacks. And what about you? Interested in meadows?'

'Yes, we just wanted to look around.'

'How brisk you are,' the old man laughed. 'I've lived around these parts for seventy years, in the same meadow, and still haven't seen it all. Just go along that path towards the black poplar. No farther, mind! If you go farther, you'll find grass as high as your head, and you'll get such a soaking from the dew that you'll be all day long getting dry again. You can fill a narrow-necked flask with that dew and drink it.'

'Have you drunk it?' asked the pilot.

'Drunk it? Of course I've drunk it. It's medicinal.'

Masha walked slowly along the path with the pilot. She took a few steps to the place where the path skirted the dried-up black poplar and stopped. On either side of the path stood high, steep walls of dog-rose, blooming with such a damp, purple fire that even the early rays of the sun, which fell upon the leaves, seemed cold and pale in comparison with the flowers. It seemed that the flowers of the dog-rose were forever separated from the thorn-branches, and were suspended in the air like small, bright flames. In the dog-rose thickets, bumble-bees buzzed anxiously, black with gold stripes on their backs.

'Knights of the George Cross,' remarked the pilot.

And really the bees did resemble the short ribbons of the George Cross medal. Like old warriors, they held themselves up courageously, paying no attention to people, only irritated by them.

Here and there, the dog-rose thickets were interrupted, and in the glades blossomed larkspur, dark blue almost bordering on black, standing like well-fashioned candles. Behind them with indescribable lush density, flowing like ripples of sunshine, rose up expanses of wild grasses, red and white clovers, cheese-rennet, snowy marguerites, wild mallows with their pink petals transparent in the light, and hundreds of other flowers for which neither Masha nor the pilot knew a name. Quails shot up with a crack from underneath their feet. Taking cover in the snags, a landrail squealed, making fun of everybody. The larks shot up quivering, but somehow their sound did not coincide with the place where they twisted and turned in the sky, but rather seemed to emanate from the river. And there, clearing its throat, the steamer whistled, summoning Masha and the pilot back.

'What's that?' said Masha perplexed, gazing at the flowers. 'What's that. . . ?'

Hurriedly she tore off armfuls of flowers with both her hands. The steamer whistled again, already anxious and angry.

'What's going on?' she said with disappointment, turning round to where the smoke was streaming from the steamer's funnel over the thickets and shouting, 'Hold on! We're coming, we're coming!'

They quickly made for the steamer. Masha's dress

was wet and clung to her legs. Her hair, which had been arranged on the back of her head in a bun, untwined and fell loose. The pilot followed, managing on the way to cut off a few flowering dog-rose branches with his knife.

The sailors, who had been waiting for them so that they could take up the gangway, cursorily glanced at the armfuls of flowers and said, 'Look at that! They've cleaned out the whole meadow! Come on! Let's get going, Semyon.'

From the bridge the captain's mate called, 'Bring the flowers into the saloon. For all the passengers . . .' and he shouted into his megaphone, 'Slow speed ahead!' The wheels turned heavily, the paddles made the water foam, and the shore swam away, noisily ruffling its shrubs.

Masha was sorry to be torn away from that shore, from the meadows with the hut and the old basket weaver. It seemed that everything had become at once dear to her, almost as if she had been born there; the old fellow might have been her foster-father or her mentor. 'Amazing!' thought Masha, hauling herself up the steps to the saloon. 'Especially as I don't even know where we are or in what region, in what district or near what town.'

In the saloon it was clean and cold. The sun had not yet warmed the polished wooden walls, the tables and the walnut piano.

Masha began to separate the flowers and arrange them in vases. The pilot brought some fresh water in a bucket from the lower deck.

'At my mum's place in Byelozyorsk,' said the pilot, helping Masha to arrange the flowers, 'there's a small garden. But even so, there are piles of flowers, especially African marigolds.'

'Did you have a good rest in Byelozyorsk?' asked Masha.

'Not bad. Read a bit. Got my life in order. There's not much else to do in Byelozyorsk.'

'What do you mean "in order"?' said Masha surprised.

'I wrote up everything I did and saw and thought. Then I considered whether I was living in the right way, what mistakes I'd made, and gave some thought to what life had presented me with recently.'

'Then what?'

'Well, now all that has happened before is straight, I can go on living with a clear head.'

'I didn't even know that it happens like that,' remarked Masha and looked attentively at the pilot.

'Well, try it some time,' the pilot advised her with a smile. 'You'll be surprised yourself just how full your life will seem.'

'Bravo!' said a familiar voice behind Masha's back.

Masha turned round.

At the doors stood the actor with a soft towel over his shoulder. He was wearing blue pyjamas with brown cuffs on the sleeves. 'Bravo!' he repeated. 'I like morning conversations. In the morning our thoughts are as fresh as newly washed hands.'

'Give it a rest,' said the pilot, a bit displeased.

'Yes, I know it's all nonsense,' the actor agreed. 'But there's no need to take it like that. I happened to overhear your conversation and I wanted to add just one detail, one irrefutable truth. I stumbled against it, you might say, at the very end of my life.'

'And what's this great truth?' asked the pilot.

'*I do not like your irony,*" said the actor in the unnatural, smarmy voice of a bad reader, and laughed. 'It's a simple truth that in every day of our life there's something good, and even something poetic. And when, as you were so kind to point out, you put your life in order, whether you wish it or not, you chiefly remember its reasoned and poetic content. That's wonderful! And amazing! Everything around us is full of poetry. Look

for it! That's my old-man's advice to you for all time.
Don't object! The conversation is ended.'

The actor left, laughing to himself, and Masha
reflected that in reality all that surrounded her here
was very simple, and at the same time quite unusual.
At the Leningrad Institute this had not been as obvious
as it was now on this journey. Perhaps it was that part
of poetry, which had been hidden before and which was
now being revealed to her, that part which is contained
in every day of existence.

On the Volga, the wind blew every day. The blueness
of the air, playing on the waves, flew over the river and
the sides of the steamer. It seemed to Masha that the
breeze was setting before her each of those summer
days, one after the other. In the evening, the wind would
drop; the river led its waters from darkness to darkness.
Only the lamps of the steamer snatched up a small
circle of illuminated water from the blackness around.
Masha felt good, and at times sad. In no way could she
believe that her new life which was starting so well
might end otherwise.

At Kamyshin, Masha disembarked. The wind brought
a yellow haze over the Volga. The pilot and the actor
were there on the jetty to bid her farewell.

A little confused, Masha waved goodbye to the pilot.
He did not quite know what to do; returning to the
steamer, he stood on the side of the boat and watched
the actor taking his leave of Masha.

The actor took off his hat, took Masha by the hands
and looked into her face with screwed up, laughing
eyes. 'You'll be happy,' he said. 'But my happiness is
greater than yours, because I'm an old man.'

'What are you talking about?' said Masha.

'You can't possibly understand the kind of happiness
given to the elderly,' said the actor bombastically. 'The
happiness of seeing tears in the eyes of a Desdemona
in love with another!' He let go of Masha's hands and

holding his hat in his hands stepped back to the gang-way. The steamer gave a third blast on its whistle and sailed away.

The breeze from the river, smelling of oil, hit her in the face. A short old man with grey whiskers was stamping his feet near Masha saying in a low voice, 'Shall I bring your things along, citizen?' But Masha neither listened to nor answered him. The little old man sat down on a wooden bench on one side and lit up, waiting patiently for Masha to calm down.

Within a day, Masha was living far away from Kamy-shin in a little wagon parked on the steppe near a pond with bare clay banks. In that mobile home which they referred to as the 'pub' were lodged two other workers on the collective forestry plant.

The boss of the plot did not turn out at all to be dusty and sullen; on the contrary he was a lively and jovial person. But from the first day of Masha's arrival, the mood on the plot was uneasy. They were all worried about whether the acorns which had been despatched to the collective would germinate or not. They were anxious about the hot dry wind which was approaching from the south-east; and over the Volga hung a glassy mist on the horizon. The words 'saline soil' were repeated over and over. Saline soil was the most impor-tunate and dangerous enemy of a young forest – those dead lichens on the steppe, that yellow clay glinting on the fractures with the white gleam of salt.

One day, taking the advice of the pilot, Masha reviewed her life and concluded that it was sharply divided into three parts: her life in Leningrad, her jour-ney on the steamer and her work on the Volga steppe. In each of these divisions she found her own good 'con-tent' and, as the old actor had said, 'poetry'.

In Leningrad there had been her room from which she could see the sunset over the seaside suburb of Lakhta; there were her girlfriends, the Institute, her books, the theatres and the parks. On her journey she had understood for the first time the joy of fleeting encounters, which had deeply touched her soul, and the charm of Russia with its free and easy rivers. And now, here on the steppe, she had come to know the great concept and power of her own work. And somewhere in the very depths of her heart, the memory of the pilot was still alive – his shy smile when he complained about the nightingales, and the way he had looked at her in Kamyshin from the deck of the steamer, and his cheek had twitched as it had done in Byelozyorsk. A man had passed by and that was a great pity.

She remembered that journey so often that one day she even dreamed about it. She dreamed of the thick bed of dog-roses in the dew. It was dusk. A young, soft moon, like a silver sickle forgotten by a reaper, lay on the dark blue coverlet of the night. So still and restful it was in her heart that Masha even laughed in her sleep . . .

The wooded plots by the soft green river poured over the hillocks and disappeared through the dry steppe where the reddish dust hung like smoke over the wide roads.

There was a lot of work to do. She had to loosen the soil between the young oaks and plant acacias. Masha took great pains over this, even showing gentle care to the young trees. She became tanned and her long hair was bleached by the sun. She now began to look like a girl from the steppe. Her dress, her hands, everything around her was permeated with the smell of wormwood, the same smell which came from the soft fur of the black watchdog, Narzan, which guarded the wagon when her colleagues had gone off to work.

The two of them looked after the wagon – Narzan and Styopa, the seven-year-old son of the boss of the plot. All day long, they both sat in the shade of the wagon listening to the whistling of the gophers and the sound of the wind in the crooked wild-pear tree, which rang so strongly it might have been cast from bronze.

Towards the end of the summer, the jerboas came and invaded the plantation. They dug holes near the oaks and wriggled around in the dust to rid themselves of fleas. The 'market garden' plane was called from Stalingrad to spread poisoned oats for them on the plantation.

One evening, when Styopa was sitting on the steps of the wagon peeling potatoes, Narzan lifted up his head and growled. Over the steppe from the direction of the setting sun a small aeroplane, its engines rumbling lazily, was flying low. It approached over the wagon, banked steeply and landed on the dry grass. Running forward a few yards, it came to a halt.

The pilot got out of the cockpit, and taking off his helmet, walked towards the wagon. He was still young but his temples were already grey. On his jacket, Styopa noticed two rows of medal-ribbons. Instead of barking at the pilot, Narzan crawled under the wagon and began to growl out of habit.

'Hello there, young fellow!' said the pilot. He sat down on the steps next to Styopa and started to smoke. 'Is this Plantation 15?'

'Yes,' said Styopa timidly. 'You've got business with us?'

'With you. I'm going to poison the jerboas.'

'You've got so many medals,' said Styopa pensively, 'and you're poisoning jerboas? We thought they'd send us the student-pilot.'

'Well, I specially asked to be sent here, my boy,' said the pilot and fell silent for a moment. 'Does Masha Klimova work here?'

'Here,' answered Styopa, narrowing his eyes. 'What of it?'

'And where is she?'

'There in the forest.' Styopa pointed in the direction of the plantation.

'Really? The forest,' the pilot smiled. He got up and without looking round went off in the direction he had been shown.

Styopa followed him with his eyes, but it had already got dark, and the steppe was hardly visible. Styopa, however, saw Masha coming from the steppe. The pilot walked quickly to meet her, but Masha did not get to him. She stopped and covered her face with her hands.

Now it was already quite dark. Over the pond, looking down at the black water from its great height, hung the wandering star of the steppe.

'Why had Masha hidden her face?' thought Styopa, and repeated the words that his father often jokingly used about Masha – 'She's an amazing girl!'

And Narzan growled all night at the plane from under the wagon, peacefully dozing on the dry, warm earth.

1951

The Dreamer

It was a month since Anfisa had finished her ten years at secondary school. The future was still uncertain. Her father, Nikolai Nikitich, would have liked Anfisa to go to Moscow and to enter the Timiryazev Agricultural Academy, but Anfisa was thinking of something quite different – still vague, but something wonderful: the theatre, travel . . .

She read books and often imagined herself to be in some strange land. So clearly she saw herself disembarking in the early morning on to the shore of this land; she left her footprints on the wet sand, and in each of them hid a small dark shadow, because the sun had just risen and its light fell obliquely on to the earth. In the distance she could see the hazy, steep slopes of lilac mountains, and cold waterfalls tumbled down them, crashing noisily into the dust.

Almost every day, Anfisa went to the town library to change her books. The library was situated on the main street, next to the new cinema. It occupied the lower storey of a brick building. It smelt of ink. The painted floors were well trodden and on the wall hung the rules for visitors and a typewritten news-sheet decorated with coloured pencils. The whole scene induced boredom, but the first impression was deceptive. Anfisa knew what treasures of poetry and thought lay hidden on the library shelves. Just recalling them sent her head into a whirl.

Her thirst for books was insatiable; she devoured them page after page, tucking herself away in her father's garden, in the dark arbour which resembled a hut made of branches and was covered with wild vines.

'Anfisa, you're spoiling your eyes!' Nikolai Nikitich would call out from the garden. He pottered about the whole day among his apple and plum trees.

'I'm coming,' said Anfisa without much enthusiasm. 'I'll just get up to the next chapter.'

'I don't want you,' Nikolai Nikitich would reply more tenderly. 'Silly girl! You'll regret your eyes. They'll fade and look like tin saucers.'

But in spite of his misgivings, Anfisa's eyes, far from going dim, with every interesting book looked even brighter and darker; sometimes they filled with tears, sometimes they shone with laughter and sometimes they clouded over, seeing nothing nearby, as if she were gazing into the distance at something disappearing beyond the edge of the world.

'She's a dreamer,' thought Nikolai Nikitich. 'She'll have it hard. I can't bear to think about it. Oh, how hard it will be for her!'

He worried about Anfisa's future, and one day went to seek advice from Nina Porfiryevna Yevseyeva, the municipal doctor, an elderly lady of firm opinions, who was devoid of any sentiment.

Nikolai Nikitich was a gardener of many years' standing and thought of himself as a 'practical kind of chap'. His one desire was to protect Anfisa from all that was superficial in life, and what he regarded as superficial was her aspiration to become an actress and her enthusiasm for poetry and novels. That all seemed to him far too colourful and smart, too likely to wither, as some flowers which fall before they have time to bloom properly. The poppy, for instance. It takes only the slightest breeze to scatter its petals on the ground, and within the hour they are dried-up, lying in the dust by the fence. Well, of course, it went without saying that Anfisa looked cut out for the theatre: a well-built girl, slim, with a voice that would take your breath away. And her hair hung down to the ground. But that was not the point!

'I can't understand it,' said Nikolai Nikitich to Nina Porfiryevna. 'I don't know who she takes after. Her mother was a good housewife, and I'm a man with plenty of common sense. I admire qualities in people that give positive results.'

'She takes after you!' answered Nina Porfiryevna, irritably.

'What do you mean? I don't understand,' said Nikolai Nikitich in amazement. 'I'm a gardener, and I want her to be one as well. There's only one thing she thinks about – the theatre, the theatre! And what's the good of that – going on the stage and just amusing people?'

'So you're a gardener,' said Nina Porfiryevna in a tone of objection. 'But why do you grow flowers? You've a garden full of them, and you've just brought me a lovely bunch.'

'Well, something pretty to look at,' explained Nikolai Nikitich, not quite sure of himself. 'Just look at these colours – everything from red to blue and gold! You won't find many flowers like this.'

'What do you call them?' asked Nina Porfiryevna abruptly, examining the large blooms, so light that they trembled in the breeze which entered her office from the garden.

'Nemesias. An African flower. I begged it from an older gardener when I was in Moscow. I threw myself at his feet. Just look at this one petal. The blue merges into violet, and the violet into purple.'

'So where's your positive result then?'

This unexpected question took Nikolai Nikitich unawares.

'I don't quite understand what you're asking.'

'What results do you get from these flowers? I'm sure you don't grow them to sell, do you?'

'I've never sold a flower in my life!' said Nikolai Nikitich ceremoniously. 'I make presents of them.'

'What a man you are!' said Nina Porfiryevna, taking off her pince-nez. At once her eyes lost their severity and looked tired and kind. 'You're always boasting that you were a friend of the composer, Arensky, when he lived here, but from art you demand an immediate, practical result. It is art that creates good people; it forms the human soul. That's all.'

'Well, but that is *art* ... ,' feebly objected Nikolai Nikitich.

'And the theatre? Isn't that art?' asked Nina Porfiryevna. 'What do you think? Anfisa has chosen the right path, so don't stand in her way! I'll call round one evening and have a word with her.'

Nikolai Nikitich left, still ill at ease.

It was already dusk. The lights were coming on in the town, but the quiet streets were much more brightly lit by the lamps radiating from open windows.

When Nikolai Nikitich arrived home, his house was in darkness. 'Has Anfisa gone out?' he thought. He sighed, lit his lamp and went into the garden. He needed to put some supports under the old apple tree.

Anfisa was sitting on a bench in the garden, so quietly that at first Nikolai Nikitich did not notice her. When he did catch sight of her, he started. She was sitting lifelessly, hunched up, muffled in her shawl. Nikolai Nikitich came up to her and sat at her side. Anfisa was silent.

'What's the matter, my little daughter?' he asked and put his hand on her shoulder. 'Aren't you well?'

'It's nothing,' she answered, pulling the shawl around herself more tightly . . .

'Why are you sitting in the dark?'

Anfisa turned to Nikolai Nikitich and looked into his eyes. The lamp had been placed on the ground and shone upwards on to Anfisa's face. Nikolai Nikitich frowned. Something glistened on her cheek, and like a dim light rolled down, and becoming extinguished fell in the darkness on to the sandy path.

'What's the matter with you?' said Nikolai Nikitich softly. 'Why are you crying?'

'Papa!' Anfisa threw her arms around his wrinkled neck, drawing herself to his shoulder. 'My dear old papa!'

'Now now! What is it . . .?' mumbled Nikolai Nikitich perplexed. 'Have you fallen in love with someone or are you bored?'

'No, I'm not in love. I can do so much good, papa. So much! For everyone! I know my own powers. Let me go to drama school. You'll never regret it.'

'We'll wait and see,' answered Nikolai Nikitich. 'You don't have to go tomorrow. You've still got till the autumn.'

His heart grew cold. It was clear that he would have to let her go. But how would he continue to live here, working in his garden, without Anfisa? Better to throw up everything, to go with her and live with her there, in Moscow.

'I don't understand the youth of today . . .' said Nikolai Nikitich quietly.

Anfisa hugged him more tightly.

'Stop that, silly girl!' said Nikolai Nikitich in a stern voice, but his head was in a whirl. 'I might even come with you.'

But it took Anfisa quite some time to pull herself together. Only when the breeze blew from the river and brought its coolness to her damp eyes did she get up, and holding tightly to her father she went with him into the house. She had to prepare the old man's dinner.

1946

Streams Where the Trout Leap

The fortunes of a certain Napoleonic marshal – we shall not mention his name for fear of angering historians and pedants! – deserve to be related especially to you, who complain of the poverty of human relations.

The marshal was still young. His greying temples and the scar on his cheek enhanced the attractiveness of his face, which had become dark from the deprivations he had suffered during the campaigns he had fought.

The soldiers loved their marshal; he had shared the hardships of battle with them. He frequently slept by the camp-fire in the fields, wrapped in his waterproof, and woke to the strident blast of the trumpet. He drank with his soldiers from the same canteen and wore a threadbare uniform which was covered in dust. He had seen nothing and knew nothing apart from tiresome marches and exhausting campaigns. He had never once thought of leaning down from the saddle and casually asking a peasant the name of the grass being trampled by his horse, or of finding out why the cities, which had been captured by his soldiers for the glory of France, were renowned. War without interruption had taught him to hold his tongue and to pay no regard to his personal life.

One day in winter, the marshal's cavalry division, which was stationed in Lombardy, received the order to proceed without delay to Germany and to join the *Grande Armée*.

On the twelfth day, the division was bivouacked in a small German town. The mountains, covered with snow, glistened in the darkness of the night. Beech woods stretched for miles around, and only rare stars twinkled in the heavens amid universal immobility.

The marshal put up at an inn. After taking a modest supper, he sat by the fireplace in the small drawing-room and dismissed his subordinates. The silence of the small town, covered from top to bottom in snow, either reminded him of his childhood or of a recent dream which he may even not have had. The marshal knew that within a day or two the Emperor was planning a decisive campaign, and consoled himself with the thought that this unaccustomed desire for silence was necessary for him – the last rest, as it were, before the thundering hooves of the attack.

A fire induces torpor in people. Fixing his gaze on the logs blazing in the hearth, the marshal did not notice the middle-aged man with a thin bird-like face who had just come into the lounge. The stranger wore a dark blue frock-coat covered in darns. He walked over to the hearth and began to warm his chilled hands.

The marshal raised his head, and with some irritation asked, 'Who might you be, sir? How is it you arrived here so quietly?'

'I'm the musician, Baumweiss,' answered the stranger. 'I came in so cautiously because on a winter's night like this one involuntarily feels that one should move without making the slightest sound.'

The musician's face and his voice inspired sympathy, and after a moment's reflection the marshal said, 'Come and sit by the fire, sir. To tell you the truth, such peaceful evenings as this are rare occurrences in my life, and I am glad to have the opportunity of talking to you.'

'I am obliged to you,' answered the musician, 'but if you don't mind, I would rather sit at the piano and play for a while. For the last two hours, I've had a tune on my mind. I need to work it out, and upstairs in my room I have no piano.'

'Of course . . .' said the marshal. 'Though the silence of the night is incomparably preferable even to the most heavenly sounds.'

Baumweiss sat down before the piano and played almost inaudibly. It seemed to the marshal that the deep, light snow which surrounded the town was almost humming, as if the winter was singing in unison with the heavily laden branches of the beech trees, and even as if the fire in the hearth was lending its voice in accompaniment. The marshal frowned, looked hard at the logs in the hearth and realized that the vibration came not from the fire but from the spurs on his high-boots.

'My imagination is already beginning to run riot with me,' said the marshal. 'You must be an extraordinary musician.'

'No,' said Baumweiss, and stopped playing. 'I only perform at the weddings and parties of minor princes and gentry.'

At the porch was a screech of sleigh-runners and the neighing of horses. Baumweiss stood up. 'Well, that's it! They've come to fetch me. Please allow me to take leave of you.'

'Where are you going?' asked the marshal.

'In the forest, a couple of leagues from here lives a forest warden,' answered Baumweiss. 'At this moment, our charming singer, Maria Czerny, is a guest in his house. She's taken refuge there from the vicissitudes of war. Today, Maria Czerny has her twenty-third birthday and she is arranging a small celebration. And how do you think they can celebrate without old Baumweiss to give them a tune?'

The marshal got up from his armchair. 'Sir,' he said, 'my division is leaving here tomorrow morning. Would I be presuming too much if I asked to join you and spend the night with you in the forest warden's house?'

'Just as you please,' answered Baumweiss, bowing with reserve, but it was noticeable that he was surprised by the marshal's question.

'But not a word to anyone,' said the marshal. 'I'll come out by the back-porch and get on the sleigh by the well.'

'Just as you please,' Baumweiss repeated his words, bowed once more and went out of the room.

The marshal smiled. That evening, he had drunk no wine, but he was overwhelmed by an unaccustomed feeling of carefree intoxication.

'To winter!' he said to himself. 'The devil take it! To the forests, to the mountains of the night! Wonderful!'

He threw on his waterproof and, without being noticed, left the inn by the garden. The sleigh was standing by the well; Baumweiss was waiting for the marshal. The snorting horses carried them past the sentry at the town gate. The sentry, out of habit, even though a bit late, presented arms and gave the marshal a salute. For a long time, he listened to the sleighbells going off into the distance, shook his head and thought, 'What a night! I'd give anything for a mouthful of mulled wine.'

The horses raced over the ground which gleamed like forged silver. The snow melted on their warm muzzles. The frost cast a spell over the woods. The black ivy clung tightly to the trunks of the beeches as if trying to give warmth to their life-giving sap. Suddenly the horses came to a halt by a stream which had not iced over. It foamed and roared across the stones, rushing from mountain caverns and dense forests, choked by wind-toppled trees and frozen leaves.

The horses were drinking from the river when something darted in the river from under their hooves like a glittering in the current. They shied and set off at full gallop along the narrow road.

'A trout,' said the coachman. 'A jolly fish.'

The marshal smiled. His feeling of intoxication had not passed and was still with him when the horses pulled the sleigh into an opening in the forest which led up to an old house with a high roof. The windows were brightly lit. The coachman jumped down and drew back the rugs.

The door opened wide and the marshal, arm in arm with Baumweiss, cast off his waterproof and approached a room which had a low ceiling and was illuminated by candles; they stopped at the threshold. In the room were a number of smartly dressed men and women.

One of the women stood up. The marshal looked at her and guessed that she must be Maria Czerny. 'Forgive me,' said the marshal with a slight blush. 'Forgive my unsolicited intrusion. But we are soldiers. We know nothing of families, celebrations or peacetime festivities. Be good enough to allow me to warm myself for a while by your fire.'

The old forester bowed to the marshal, and Maria Czerny hastily walked towards him, fixed him with her eyes and held out her hand. The marshal kissed her hand, which seemed to him as cold as ice. All fell silent. Maria Czerny carefully touched the marshal's cheek and pointed to the deep scar. 'Was it very painful?' she asked.

'Yes,' he answered with some embarrassment. 'It was a sharp blow from a sabre.'

Then she took his hand and led him towards the guests. She introduced him to them coyly and radiantly, as if she already regarded him as her fiancé. Whispers of perplexity spread among the assembled company.

I wonder, my dear reader, whether there is any need for me to give you a description of Maria Czerny. If, like me, you had lived in her time, you would surely have heard of the dazzling beauty of that woman, of her elegant gait, of her capricious yet captivating disposition. There was not one man who dared hope to win the love of Maria Czerny. It may be that only those rare people like Schiller could have been worthy of her love.

And then what happened? The marshal stayed for two days in the house of the forester. Let us not talk of love, because to this very day we have not discovered its true nature. Could it have been the dense snow which fell all night, or the winter streams where the trout leap? Could it have been the laughter and the song, and the smell of old resin before the dawn, when the candles are burning low and the stars come closer to the window-panes in order to twinkle in the eyes of Maria Czerny?

Who knows? Perhaps even the bare hand on the hard shoulder, the fingers stroking the cold hair, the darned frock-coat of Baumweiss; the tears of a man shed for what his heart never expected – tenderness, caresses, disjointed whispers among the forests of the night. Perhaps even the return of childhood. Who knows? Could it have been the despair before saying goodbye, when the heart sinks and Maria Czerny fitfully glides her hands over the wallpaper, over the tables and the leaves of the door of the room which was a witness to her love? Finally it might be the cry and the swooning of a woman, when outside in the smoke of the torches, to the clipped shouts of command, the Napoleonic gendarmerie dismount from their saddles and march into the house in order to arrest the marshal at the personal bidding of the Emperor.

There are stories which flash by and are gone like

birds, but remain for ever in the memory of those who have involuntarily witnessed them.

Everything around remained as before. The woods groaned as they always groaned when the wind blew, and the stream, with its small eddies, engulfed the dark fallen leaves. The sound of the axe echoed in the mountains and women gossiped in the town as they gathered at the well.

But somehow the woods and the fluttering snow and the gleam of the leaping trout in the stream caused Baumweiss to take out from the back pocket of his frock-coat an old but snowy-white handkerchief, to bring it to his eyes and to whisper incoherent, sad words about the brief love of Maria Czerny and how at times life resembles music.

But, Baumweiss whispered, in spite of the heartache, that he was glad he had been part of this incident, and had experienced an emotion which had so rarely fallen to the lot of the old hack-pianist.

1939

Rainy Dawn

The steamer arrived in Navoloki at night. Major Kuzmin came out on to the deck. It was drizzling and the jetty was deserted – only one lamp was burning.

'Where can the town be?' thought Kuzmin. 'Darkness, rain – to hell with it!'

He shivered and buttoned up his overcoat around him. A cold wind blew from the river. Kuzmin sought the help of the captain's assistant and asked him how long the steamer would be stopping in Navoloki.

'About three hours,' he answered. 'But why do you ask? You're going farther, aren't you?'

'I've got a letter to deliver, from a workmate of mine in the military hospital. It's for his wife. She lives here in Navoloki.'

'You've got a problem!' sighed the assistant. 'You can't see a hand in front of your face. You'd better listen out for the whistle, otherwise you'll be left behind.'

Kuzmin stepped on to the jetty and climbed the slippery flight of steps up the steep bank. He could hear the rain pelting against the bushes. He stood there for a while, letting his eyes grow accustomed to the dark, and caught sight of a miserable-looking horse and a slanting dog-cart. The hood was up, and the sound of snoring came from beneath it.

'Hey, friend! You'll sleep your life away!' Kuzmin called loudly.

The coachman turned over, lifted himself up, blew his nose and wiped it on the hem of his coarse-cloth shirt. Only then he asked: 'You want to go somewhere?'

'Yes, I do,' said Kuzmin.

'Where do you want me to take you?'

Kuzmin named the street.

'It's a long way,' said the coachman, a bit worried. 'On the hill. It'll cost you at least a quarter of vodka.' He tugged on the reins, clicking his tongue. The cab moved off reluctantly.

'Are you the only cabman in Navoloki?' asked Kuzmin.

'No. There are two. Both of us old men. The rest have joined up. Whose house do you want?'

'Bashilov's.'

'I know,' answered the cabman with animation, turning round to look at Kuzmin. 'Olga Andreyevna's place – the daughter of the doctor, Andrei Petrovich. She came from Moscow last winter and settled in her father's house. It must be two years since Andrei Petrovich died, but his house . . .'

The cab rocked, clanked and bounced out of a pit in the road.

'You watch where you're going,' advised Kuzmin. 'Don't keep looking back.'

'This road really is . . .' mumbled the cabman. 'If you went along it during the day, you'd be scared. But at night, it's nothing. At night, you can't see the potholes.'

The cabman fell silent. Kuzmin lit a cigarette and withdrew himself into the depths of the coach. The rain beat down on to the hood above. The dogs were barking in the distance. There was a smell of dill, wet fences, dampness from the river. 'One o'clock at least,' thought Kuzmin. And at that very moment, a cracked bell in a clock-tower somewhere actually struck one!

'It would be good to spend the whole leave here,' mused Kuzmin. 'Just breathing the air of the place would soothe all the pains of the wounds. Just to rent a room in a little house with windows looking out on to the garden. To have the windows wide open on a night like this, to lie in bed under the blankets and listen to the rain beating against the burdocks.'

'You're not her husband, are you?' asked the cabman.

Kuzmin did not answer. The cabman thought that the soldier had not heard his question, but did not dare to ask again. 'Must be her husband,' he concluded. 'And people gossip and say she threw her husband over even before the war. I suppose it's all lies.'

'Come on, gee up, you devil,' he shouted, cracking the reins down on to the back of the bony horse. 'Come on, get on with it!'

'It's stupid that the steamer was late and arrived at night,' thought Kuzmin. Why had Bashilov – his neighbour in the hospital ward – as soon as he had found out that Kuzmin would be passing through Navoloki, asked him to give a letter to his wife, personally and without fail? Waking people up in the middle of the night! God knows what they would think of him!

Bashilov was a tall, jovial officer. He enjoyed conversation, and talked a lot. Before making a pointed remark, he would laugh to himself for a long time without a sound. He had been an assistant to a film producer before joining the army, and every evening would give detailed accounts of the most outstanding films to his fellow patients. The wounded soldiers loved his stories, looked forward to them and marvelled at his memory.

Bashilov was scathing in his judgements on people, events and books; he was a very obstinate man, and poured ridicule on anyone who tried to contradict him. But his ridicule was subtle, made by insinuation and jest, and usually it was an hour or two before the person who had been its object suddenly realized that Bashilov

had offended him, and, obviously, when he had thought
up a suitably venomous answer, it was already too late
to snap back.

The day before Kuzmin was due to depart, Bashilov
handed him the letter he had written to his wife and,
for the first time, Kuzmin detected in his face a smile
of perplexity. During the night, he had heard Bashilov
turning over in bed and sniffing. 'Perhaps, after all, he
does have feelings,' thought Kuzmin. 'It sounds as if
he is crying. That means he's in love. Deeply in love.'

The whole of the next day, Bashilov would not leave
Kuzmin alone. He kept looking at him, made him a
present of his officer's flask, and a few moments before
the departure they drank a bottle of wine that Bashilov
had specially prepared.

'What are you looking at me like that for?' asked
Kuzmin.

'You're a good fellow,' answered Bashilov. 'You could
have been an artist, my dear major.'

'I'm a topographer,' answered Kuzmin. 'And topogra-
phers are by their nature the same as artists.'

'Why?'

'They're wanderers,' Kuzmin answered vaguely.

'Exiles, wanderers and poets,' declared Bashilov with
a touch of irony, 'who aspired but succeeded in nothing.'

'Where's that from?'

'A verse of Voloshin.[8] But that's nothing to do with
it. I look at you because I envy you. That's all.'

'Why on earth should you envy me?'

Bashilov turned the glass around in his fingers, leant
back in his chair and smiled. They were sitting by a
wicker table at the end of the hospital corridor. Outside,
the wind was bending the young saplings, rustling the
leaves and stirring up the dust. From the river a rainy
mist was heading towards the town.

'Why do I envy you?' Bashilov echoed the question

and placed his red hand on Kuzmin's. 'I envy you for everything. Even for your hand.'

'I don't understand you,' said Kuzmin, carefully withdrawing his hand. He found Bashilov's cold touch unpleasant, but in order that Bashilov should not notice anything, he took the bottle and began to pour the wine.

'So you don't understand!' Bashilov answered angrily. He was silent for a while and then spoke, lowering his eyes. 'If only we could swap places! But, of course, that's all nonsense. In a day or two, you'll be in Navoloki. You'll see Olga Andreyevna. She'll shake your hand. That's why I envy you. Now do you understand?'

'Oh, come on!' said Kuzmin, confused. 'You'll see your wife as well.'

'She's not my wife!' said Bashilov harshly. 'It's just as well that you didn't call her my "lawful spouse"!'

'Sorry,' Kuzmin mumbled.

'She's not my wife,' repeated Bashilov with the same abruptness. 'She's everything to me. She's my life. Anyway, that's enough of that.' He stood up and offered Kuzmin his hand: 'Goodbye, and don't be angry with me. I'm no worse than the others.'

The cab reached the dike. The darkness grew more intense. There was a sleepy rustling in the old willows and the rain trickled from the leaves. The horse's hooves clattered on the planks of the bridge.

'It's quite a long way,' sighed Kuzmin, and called to the cabman. 'Wait for me by the house. You can take me back to the jetty . . .'

'I'll do that,' agreed the cabman at once and thought: 'No, it can't be her husband. The husband would be sure to stay for a day or two. He's obviously a stranger.'

They drove along the cobbled road. The cab was shuddering; its iron footboards rattled. The driver pulled over to the side. The wheels rolled softly in the sand. Kuzmin sank once more into his reverie.

Bashilov had been envious of him. It was surely not

envy. Bashilov had simply used the wrong word. On
the contrary, after the conversation by the window in
the hospital, it was Kuzmin who envied Bashilov.
'Wrong again!' said Kuzmin to himself with vexation.
He was not envious. He was just sorry. Sorry because
he was already forty and he had never experienced the
kind of love that Bashilov had known. He had always
been by himself.

'Night rain is beating down over the empty gardens;
a strange town, mist rising from the meadows – that's
how life will pass by,' the thought occurred to Kuzmin.

Once more he felt the desire to stay. He loved small
Russian towns, where you could see the meadows from
the porch across the river, the wide roads ascending the
hill and carts on the ferry-boats piled high with hay.
He was surprised by his affection himself. He had grown
up in the south, born to a seafaring family. From his
father he had inherited his love for investigation, atlases
and wandering. That is why he had become a topographer. He regarded his choice of profession as purely
fortuitous, and thought that if he had been born in
another age, he might have been a hunter or a pioneer
opening up new lands. He liked to think of himself in
these terms, but he was mistaken. There was nothing
in his character that was peculiar to such people.
Kuzmin was retiring and gentle with those around him.
Light grey streaks in his hair betrayed his age, but no
one who looked at this slightly-built, average-sized
officer would have given him more than thirty.

At last, the cab entered the dark town. Only one
building – probably a chemist's – was lit by a blue light,
burning behind a glass-panelled door. The street led up
a hill. The cabman climbed down from his seat to make
it easier for his horse. Kuzmin got down as well. He
walked slowly, trailing behind the cab, and suddenly
became aware of the strangeness of his own life. 'Where
am I?' he thought. 'Some place called Navoloki, a back-

water; sparks are flying from the horseshoes; and somewhere nearby is a woman I don't know. In the middle of the night, I've got to hand her an important letter, and, for all I know, not a very pleasant one. A few years ago, we were at the front – Poland and the broad, quiet Wisla. Strange somehow. Still, you feel well!'

They reached the top of the hill and the cabman turned into a sidestreet. Somewhere overhead, the clouds parted and, amid the blackness, now and then, a solitary star glimmered, reflected its light in the puddles and then was extinguished.

The cab stopped by a house with an attic. 'Here we are,' said the cabman. 'The bell's by the gate on the right.'

Kuzmin groped for the wooden handle of the bell, found it and tugged. But there was no sound except the twang of rusty barbed wire.

'Pull harder,' advised the cabman.

Kuzmin once more pulled the handle. The muffled tinkling of a bell sounded from the depths of the house. As before, there was silence. No one, evidently, had woken up.

'O-O-oh!' yawned the cabman. 'A rainy night is when you sleep soundest.'

Kuzmin waited for a while and pulled the bell harder. The sound of footsteps was heard in the wooden passage. Someone approached the door, stopped, listened and called out irritably. 'Who is it? What do you want?'

Kuzmin was about to answer, but the cabman forestalled him.

'Open up, Marfa! Someone's come for Olga Andreyevna. From the Front.'

'Who – from the Front?' asked the same unkind voice from behind the door.

'You might not be expecting anyone, but he's here!'

The door opened on a chain. Kuzmin announced himself in the darkness and explained why he had come.

'Good heavens!' said the woman behind the door, confused. 'What a nuisance for you! I'll open up at once. Olga Andreyevna's asleep. Come in. I'll wake her up.'

The door opened and Kuzmin stepped into the dark passage.

'Mind the step,' warned the woman in a different, already more pleasant voice. 'Such a dark night you've come on. Just wait. Don't hurt yourself. I'll light the lamp. You see, we don't have it burning all night.'

She went off and Kuzmin was left standing in the passage. From the rooms wafted the scent of tea and a more indefinable, pleasant smell. A cat emerged into the passage, rubbed itself against Kuzmin's legs, purred and went back into the dark rooms, delivering, as it were, an invitation to join them.

There was a glimmer of dim light from behind the door. 'Please come in,' the woman said. Kuzmin entered. The woman bowed to him – a tall, elderly lady with a dark face. Trying not to make a noise, Kuzmin took off his overcoat and cap, and hung them on the peg by the door.

'Don't fret yourself,' said the old lady, smiling. 'I have to wake Olga Andreyevna up anyway.'

'Can you hear the boat's whistle from here?' asked Kuzmin in a low voice.

'Of course you can, my dear. You'll hear it easily. So, you're from the steamer! There you are. Sit here on the divan.'

The old woman left the room. Kuzmin sat down on the divan with a wooden back, hesitated a moment, took out a cigarette and lit it. He was anxious without knowing why, and this irritated him. He was overcome by the sort of feeling you always experience when you find yourself in a strange house at night, making an intrusion into someone else's life, full of mystery and conjecture. This life is like a book, lying forgotten on a table, open at page sixty-five. You glance at the page, and try to guess who wrote the book, and what it is about.

There was in fact a book lying open on the table. Kuzmin got up, bent over it and, aware of the sound of hurried whispering behind the door and the rustling of a dress, read to himself words he had long forgotten:[9]

> The impossible becomes possible,
> The distant road grows light,
> When a momentary glance from under a scarf
> Flashes in the far-off night.

Kuzmin lifted his eyes and looked around. The low, warm room once again stirred him with the desire to stay in this small town.

There is a peculiar, simple comfort in rooms such as these, with a lamp covered in a white, matt shade, hanging over the dining-table, a stag's horns above a picture depicting a dog standing by the bed of a sick girl. Such rooms, all so old-fashioned, so long ago forgotten, make you smile.

Everything around, even the pink shell ashtray, spoke of life, peaceful and long, and once more Kuzmin thought how good it would have been to stay and live like the inhabitants of the old house, unhurried, alternating work with rest, winter with spring, days of rain with days of sun.

But among the old things in the room there were others. On the table was a bunch of meadow-flowers – camomile, lungwort, wild rowan-berries. These flowers must have been picked recently, for there were paring knives on the tablecloth and discarded stems which had been clipped off by them. At their side lay an open volume of Blok's verse, *The Distant Road is Light*, and on the piano, placed on top of a blue plush photograph album, was a small, black lady's hat, not at all old-fashioned, but very much *à la mode*. And carelessly thrown on the table was a small watch with a nickel bracelet. It ticked silently, and indicated half-past one. And a little sad, as it always is, especially so late at night, was the scent of perfume.

One window-shutter was open. Behind the shutter and the pots of begonias on the sill, a wet lilac bush was glittering from the dim light which fell on it from the window. The drizzle whispered in the darkness, and heavy drops of water hurriedly pounded on the tin gutter. Kuzmin listened to the rain dripping. The thought that has tormented people for centuries of the impossibility of capturing each passing moment went through his mind, just now, at night, in a strange house, from which in the space of a few minutes he would depart, never to return.

'I must be getting old,' thought Kuzmin as he turned round. At the door stood a young woman in a black dress. She had evidently been in a hurry to join him and had arranged her hair carelessly. One braid fell down on to her shoulder and, without taking her eyes off Kuzmin, the woman, with an embarrassed smile, took it up and fastened it with a pin to the hair at the back of her head. Kuzmin bowed.

'Do excuse me,' said the woman, offering her hand to Kuzmin. 'I've kept you waiting.'

'You must be Olga Andreyevna Bashilova.'

'Yes.'

Kuzmin looked at the woman. He was surprised by her youth and the gleam in her eyes – deep and slightly misty. He excused himself for the trouble he had caused, took Bashilov's letter from his jacket pocket and handed it to the woman. She accepted the letter, thanked him and without reading it, placed it on the piano.

'So why are we standing?' she said. 'Please sit down. Here by the table. There's more light.'

Kuzmin sat at the table and asked permission to smoke.

'Please do,' said the woman. 'I might as well have one, too.'

Kuzmin offered her a cigarette and struck a match. As she lit the cigarette, the light of the match fell upon her face, and the intense face with its unlined forehead at once seemed familiar to Kuzmin.

Olga Andreyevna sat opposite him. He waited for her questions, but she kept silent, looking out of the window, where the rain fell with a monotonous sound.

'Marfusha!' called Olga Andreyevna, turning towards the door. 'Be a dear and heat the samovar up.'

'Please, there's no need,' said Kuzmin in confusion. 'I'm in a hurry. The cabman's waiting in the street. All I came to do was to give you the letter and tell you something about your . . . husband.'

'What is there to tell?' answered Olga Andreyevna, pulling a camomile flower from the bunch, and mercilessly tearing the petals from it. 'He's alive, and I'm glad.'

Kuzmin fell silent.

'Don't be impatient,' said Olga Andreyevna, exactly as if she were addressing an old friend. 'We'll hear the whistle. I'm sure the steamer won't leave before dawn.'

'Why?'

'Well, my dear,' came Marfa's voice from the neighbouring room, 'just below Navoloki there's a big sandbank in the river. It's dangerous to pass through during the night. That's why the captains always wait till dawn.'

'True,' confirmed Olga Andreyevna. 'It's only a quarter of an hour's walk to the jetty if you go through the town park. I'll see you off and send your cabman away. Who brought you? Vasily?'

'I've really no idea,' smiled Kuzmin.

'No. It was Timofey,' said Marfa from the other side

of the door, rattling the pipe of the samovar. 'Now
you'll have some tea. You've just come out of the rain;
then back into the rain.'

Kuzmin agreed, walked to the gate and paid off the
cabman. The cabman hung around, shuffled his feet by
the horse and adjusted his balaclava helmet.

When Kuzman returned, the table was already laid.
There were old blue cups with golden rims, a jug filled
with baked milk, honey and a bottle of wine, already
started. Marfa brought in the samovar.

Olga Andreyevna made excuses for the poor fare,
explained that she was intending to return to Moscow,
and in the meantime was working in the municipal
library in Navoloki. All the time, Kuzmin waited for
her to ask about Bashilov, but she did not, and for that
reason he became all the more embarrassed. Even in
the hospital, he had sensed that there was something
wrong between Bashilov and his wife, but now that she
had placed his letter on the piano without even glancing
at it, he was convinced of it, and began to feel that he
had not fulfilled his duty towards his friend, for which
he blamed himself. 'Of course, she'll read the letter
when I've gone,' he thought. However, it was obvious
that the letter to which Bashilov had given such significance, and because of which Kuzmin had appeared
in this house at such an unearthly hour, was already
unwanted here and of no interest. In the end, Kuzmin
had not helped Bashilov, but had merely put himself in
an uncomfortable position.

Olga Andreyevna seemed to have guessed, and said,
'Don't be offended. There *is* the post, there *is* a telegraph
service – I don't know why it was necessary for him to
trouble you.'

'It was no trouble,' hastily answered Kuzmin, and
after a pause added: 'On the contrary it was a great
pleasure.'

'What pleasure?'

Kuzmin reddened.

'What pleasure?' Olga Andreyevna repeated the question, and met Kuzmin's eyes. She looked at him, as if trying to guess what he was thinking – intensely, edging forward, waiting for an answer. But Kuzmin remained silent.

'But tell me, what pleasure?' she asked again.

'How can I put it?' answered Kuzmin, marshalling his thoughts. 'It's a special matter. It's seldom that everything happens to us as we would like. I don't know about others. I'm talking for myself. Everything that is pleasurable almost always passes you by. You see what I mean.'

'Not really,' answered Olga Andreyevna, with a frown.

'How can I explain it to you?' said Kuzmin, becoming angry with himself. 'You've probably experienced it as well. From a window in a train you suddenly catch a glimpse of a clearing in a birch wood. You see a spider's web glinting in the autumn sun. And you are overcome by the urge to jump out of the moving train and to remain in that clearing. But the train passes it by. You lean out of the window and look back at the passing scenery – the glades, the meadows, the horses, the cart-roads, and you hear an indefinable sound. You can't work out what is making the noise. Perhaps it is the woods or the air or the hum of the telegraph-wires. Perhaps it's the rails ringing to the movement of the train. It's there for a fleeting moment, and you remember it for the rest of your life.'

Kuzmin fell silent. Olga Andreyevna pushed a glass of wine towards him.

'In my life,' said Kuzmin, and blushed as he always did when he chanced to talk about himself, 'I have always had a longing for such unexpected and simple things. And if I have found them, I have been happy. Not for long. But I have been.'

'At this moment as well?' asked Olga Andreyevna.

'Yes.'

Olga Andreyevna lowered her eyes. 'Why?' she asked.

'I don't know exactly. It's just how I feel. I was wounded in Wisla, and lay in hospital. Everyone received letters except me. It was simply because I had no one to receive them from. I lay there, and, naturally, dreamed, like everyone else, about the future, about what I would do after the war. I was sure that it would be happy and unusual. Then I recovered and they decided to send me on leave. They even picked the town for me.'

'Which one?' asked Olga Andreyevna.

Kuzmin named the town. She said nothing in response.

'I boarded the steamer,' he continued. 'Villages on the banks, jetties. And a heavy sense of solitude. For God's sake. Don't think I'm feeling sorry for myself. In solitude there's also a great deal that's good. Then, Navoloki. I was afraid I might oversleep and miss it. At night I came out on the deck and thought how strange it was that in this vast darkness, covering the whole of Russia, thousands of different people were sleeping soundly under a rainy sky. Then I came here in the cab and wondered whom I would meet.'

'Even so, what is it that makes you so happy?' asked Olga Andreyevna.

'It's . . .' Kuzmin suddenly remembered something, 'just that it's good in general.'

He fell silent.

'Go on, tell me.'

'Tell you what? Look, I've been too talkative and I've already said more than I needed to.'

'Tell me everything,' said Olga Andreyevna. She seemed not to have heard his last words. 'Tell me what you wish,' she added. 'Though it's all a bit strange.'

She got up, went over to the window and drew back the curtain. The rain had not abated.

'Still raining,' said Olga Andreyevna, turning round. 'Meeting like this, and this conversation of ours in the middle of the night. Don't you think it strange?'

Kuzmin maintained an embarrassed silence. Outside in the damp gloom, somewhere below the town, was the sound of the steamer's whistle.

'Well, there you are,' said Olga Andreyevna with apparent relief. 'There's your whistle.'

Kuzmin got up. Olga Andreyevna did not move. 'Let's sit before taking the road. As we used to.'[10]

Kuzmin sat down again. Olga Andreyevna also sat, pensively, even turning her back on Kuzmin. Looking at her high shoulders, the heavy braids of hair pinned up at the back, the smooth curve of her neck, Kuzmin thought that if it had not been for Bashilov, he would not have left this town. He would have stayed till the end of his leave, and lived with his emotions, knowing that nearby also lived this kind and now very sad woman.

Olga Andreyevna got up. In the small hall, Kuzmin helped her on with her raincoat. She put a scarf over her head.

They went out and walked silently along the dark street.

'It will soon be dawn,' said Olga Andreyevna.

The watery sky was turning blue over the river. Kuzmin noticed that Olga Andreyevna had started to shiver.

'Are you cold?' he asked caringly. 'There was no need for you to come and see me off. I could have found the road myself.'

'Yes, there was,' answered Olga Andreyevna abruptly.

The rain stopped, but water continued to drip from the roofs, and sounded on the wooden planks of the pavement.

The town park was spread out at the end of the street. The neglected, overgrown pathway began on the other side of the gate. The park smelt of the coldness of the night and of wet sand. It was an old park, black with tall lime trees, whose flowers had already faded and gave off a vague scent. A single gust of wind blew through the garden, and everything rustled, as if a sudden, strong downpour had fallen on it and then had quickly abated. At the end of the park was a steep slope down to the river, and behind it the rainswept distance before the dawn, the dim lights of the buoys down below, the mist, and all the sadness of inclement summer weather.

'How do we get down?' asked Kuzmin.

'This way.'

Olga Andreyevna turned on to the path which led to the slope, and went towards some wooden steps leading down into the darkness.

'Give me your hand,' said Olga Andreyevna. 'Many of the steps are rotten.'

Kuzmin gave her his hand and they began to descend with care. Grass, wet from the rain, grew between the steps. They stopped on the last one. The jetty and the green and red lights of the steamer were already visible. There was a hiss of steam. Kuzmin's heart missed a beat when he realized that in a moment he would part from this woman, a stranger, but one so dear to him, and he would say nothing to her. Nothing! He would not even thank her for coming across his path, for offering him her small, firm hand in the damp glove, for bringing him down the decaying steps and, every time she saw a wet branch hanging over the railings, for saying gently, 'Keep your head down.' And Kuzmin obediently lowered his head.

'Well, I'll say goodbye here,' said Olga Andreyevna. 'I shan't come any farther.'

Kuzmin glanced at her. She was looking at him from

under her scarf with her alarmed, severe eyes. Could it really be true that now, at this very moment, everything would melt into the past and become one of those weary memories in both her life and his?

Olga Andreyevna held her hand out towards Kuzmin. He kissed it and was conscious of that same vague scent of perfume that he had first smelt in the dark room as the rain fell. When he raised his head, Olga Andreyevna said something, but so softly that he did not hear it properly. It seemed as if she had pronounced one phrase: 'To no purpose . . .' She might have said something else, but from the river, the steamer screeched its complaint against the dank light of dawn, against its life spent wandering among the mists and the rains.

Without looking round, Kuzmin hurried to the shore, crossed the jetty, which smelt of bast and tar, boarded the steamer, and at once gained its empty deck. The boat was already pulling away, its paddle-wheels slowly rotating. Kuzmin reached the stern and looked towards the slope, the steps – Olga Andreyevna was still there. It was hardly light enough to make her out. He raised his arm, but she gave no reply.

The steamer went farther and farther away, throwing long waves on to the sandy shore, rocking the buoys, and the willow bushes on the edge of the bank with a hasty sound gave answer to the beat of the steamer's paddles.

1945

The Inscription on the Boulder

For a writer complete happiness comes only when he is convinced that his conscience is found to be in accordance with the conscience of his fellow-men.

Saltykov-Shchedrin[11]

I live in a small house on the dunes. The whole of the Riga coast is under a cover of snow. All the time it flies down from the tall pines in long strands and scatters into dust. It flies down because of the wind and also because the squirrels romp around in the pines. When it is very quiet, you can even hear them peeling the pine-cones.

The house stands right on the sea. In order to get a view of the sea, you need to go out of the wicket-gate and walk a little way along the path beaten in the snow near the *dacha* which is closed for the winter.

At the windows of the *dacha*, the curtains still remain from the summer. They flap in the gentle wind. The wind probably gets into the empty house through unheeded chinks, but looking at it from far off you might imagine that someone is lifting up the curtains and carefully spying on you.

The sea has not frozen. The snow is lying up to the very edge of the water; on it are visible the tracks of hares.

When the waves get up on the sea, it is not the sound of the breakers you hear but the crunching of the ice and the rustling of the snow which is settling upon it.

In the winter, the Baltic coast is deserted and surly.

The Letts call it Dzintara Yura, the 'Amber Sea'. Perhaps not only because the Baltic yields a great deal of amber, but rather because its water is tinged with an amber yellow.

All day long, a heavy mist lies there on the horizon in layers. The outlines of the low shores are lost in it. Only here and there in the mist, white, shaggy stripes come down over the sea – there it is snowing.

Sometimes, wild geese, flying in too early this year, settle on the water and cry out. Their alarm-call carries far over the shore, but excites no response. In the winter there are hardly any birds in the woods that line the shore.

By day, in the house where I live the normal daily routine proceeds. Firewood crackles in the multi-coloured tiled stoves, there is the muffled tapping of the typewriter, and the taciturn cleaning-woman, Lilya, sits in the cosy hall knitting lace. All is as usual and very simple.

But in the evening, pitch-black darkness surrounds the house, the pines bend close up against it, and when you go outside from the brightly lit hall, you are enveloped by a sensation of complete solitude eye to eye with the earth, the sea and the night.

The sea extends for hundreds of miles into the black-leaden distance. Not one light can be seen upon it; not one splash can be heard.

The little building stands like the last lighthouse on the edge of a foggy abyss. Here the earth ends, and for that reason it seems amazing that in the house the light burns peacefully, the radio sings out, the soft carpets muffle the footsteps and on the tables books and manuscripts lie open.

There towards the west in the direction of Ventspils, behind its mist, is a small fishing settlement. An ordinary fishing settlement with nets drying in the wind, with low houses and low smoke blowing from the chimneys, with black motor-boats dragged up on to the sand, and trusty dogs with shaggy fur.

Latvian fishermen have been living in the settlement for hundreds of years. One generation replaces another. Fair-haired girls with shy eyes and melodious voices become windswept, thick-set old ladies, wrapped in heavy scarves. Bronzed youths with their foppish caps turn into bristly old men with imperturbable eyes.

In the same way as centuries ago, fishermen put out to sea for sprats, and in the same way as centuries ago, not all return. Especially in the autumn when the Baltic grows savage with storms and boils with cold foam like the cauldrons of the Devil. But no matter what happens, no matter how many times they have to take off their caps when people come to know of the death of their own comrades, even so they have to carry on their business, perilous and hard, handed down to them by their fathers and grandfathers. The sea cannot be given in to.

On the shore by the sea is a big granite boulder, on which some time ago the fishermen carved an inscription: *In Memory of All Those Who Have Perished* or *Will Perish at Sea*. The inscription can be seen from far away.

When I first saw the inscription, it seemed sad to me, like all epitaphs, but a Latvian writer talking to me about it did not agree and said, 'On the contrary. It's a very courageous inscription. It says that people will never give in, and regardless of anything will carry on with their life. I would use that inscription as a dedication for any book about human toil and persistence. For me it sounds more like: "In memory of those who have overcome and will overcome this sea." '

I agreed with him and thought that the dedication might equally well be used for a book about the labours of a writer.

Writers cannot for a moment give up before adversities and stop before obstacles. Whatever happens, they must carry on relentlessly with the work bequeathed to them by their forerunners and entrusted to them by their contemporaries. It was not for nothing that Saltykov-Shchedrin said that if literature falls silent even for a moment, that will be tantamount to the death of the people.

Writing is not a mechanical process, nor an occupation. Writing is a vocation.

When we investigate certain words, their own phonation and etymology reveal to us their original meaning. The word *vocation* comes from the Latin *vocare*, 'to call', as the Russian equivalent *prizvaniye* comes from the root *zov*, meaning the same thing. They never summon a person to 'work by rote'; they call him only to the fulfilment of a duty and an arduous problem.

What then pushes a writer to his sometimes tormenting but wonderful work?

First and foremost the call of his own heart. The voice of conscience and trust in the future do not allow the genuine writer to live on this earth like a barren flower without giving people in generous measure the whole vast and varied canvas of the thoughts and feelings of his very mind. That person who has not added even a little perspicacity to the sight of others cannot be called a writer.

A person does not become a writer only from the call of his heart. The voice of the heart is most often heard in our youth when nothing has yet clogged or torn to shreds the fresh world of our feelings.

Then come the years of maturity, and we hear more clearly something other than the invocatory voice of our own heart, a new and more powerful call – the call of our times, of our people, of our humanity.

1955

Fenya's Happiness

The train left Moscow at night. It was cramped in the carriage. We went out into the dark corridor and stood by the door to get a breath of air. The waning moon flew along, keeping pace with the train, over the tops of the birch trees in the forest through which we were passing. As always in September, a bitterly cold wind blew against the door with the smell of river water and wet leaves.

At the brief halts, the moon stopped with the train and seemed to grow brighter, probably because of the increasing silence. The engine breathed heavily and the cry of a child reached us from the carriage – children always cry at night on trains.

A woman, wearing a scarf, came out into the corridor carrying a bag. Behind her an angry female voice cried out, 'You just can't get by, and there she is swinging that bag around! Look at her! Look how the lady is swinging her arms about!'

'Leave me alone with your fine words,' answered the woman wearing the scarf, in a voice that sounded young, and closed the door behind her.

It was the first time we had travelled in these parts. The train arrived in the station late at night and neither of us knew the way. I asked the woman the way: 'Excuse me, do you know how to get to Bobylin?'

'You'll lose yourself,' answered the woman. 'The road goes through the forest. It's treacherous. I'm going as far as Suglinki myself. I'll take you there. I'm nervous of walking alone at night. And it's only three kilometres from Suglinki to Bobylin.'

There wasn't a soul at the station. A solitary electric lamp burnt in the night. At the crossing, in the entrance to a dark building, a cock flapped its wings and crowed.

We set off along the forest road. The moon was sinking behind the trees. The wheel-ruts, soaked by a recent shower, glistened in the shadows. Then the forest opened up and we emerged into the water-meadows of the River Dubna. The whole meadow, edging the groves and the forest, with the smoky mass of the grey-flecked willows on the banks, the mist spreading over the bends, the steep incline down to the river and the stars playing over the thickets, gave us the impression of a mysterious, longed-for land. It seemed to us that we were wanderers, finally approaching those far-off waters where the willow-grass of fairy stories blooms without fading, and day after day there is the blue of the sky, gossamer flying on the wind over the pastures . . .

'There you are,' said my companion, 'people dream of long summers. But I dream of a long autumn, like this, warm and misty.'

The woman laughed. 'You're right,' she said. 'It's not only you people from the city; country people like us have the same sort of desires. There are days when you just can't help feeling happy. Every ear of corn lies in the harvested field as if it had been cast in a mould. When you pick it up, it's hot from the sun. You examine it, and there's a beetle sitting on it – a bit late in the day – warming himself and twirling his moustache. In the cottage it's dry with the light from the garden – the garden always gives a yellow reflection. I wish I could go on sitting by the window and never move away. Just looking at the wild roses in the garden and thinking . . .

It's in the autumn that our water-mill starts to work and grind the corn. I'm employed in the mill; I help the miller. It's true that the mill's old, but it's no good your saying that it's only fit for the Devil to grind his tobacco in!'

'But what would you be thinking about by the window?' asked my friend.

The woman pondered for a long time and then answered in a melodious voice, 'About people's happiness. That's what we're here for.'

'Who?'

'Women.'

'Surely not just women?'

'No, probably everyone,' the woman agreed at last. 'But women more than anything are meant for that.'

'And has it ever happened to you – to bring people happiness?' asked my friend.

The woman laughed again. 'Oh! That's difficult. I can't say myself. I might have done. I know little enough about such things. You see, I'm not educated. I used to work in a pottery firm – it was called Gardeners' – and now I work in the flour-mill. Listen! Can you hear it?' she added, obviously wishing to change the subject. 'There's the sound of the water in the dam. Over there by the mill.'

We stopped and listened. Behind the dark wall of brittle-willows, where the sky had already turned green in the dawn, there was the monotonous sound of cascading water. The noise it made – the only sound in the silence of the night – bore witness to the ceaseless movement of nature. We probably all began to think of forest streams running under wind-fallen trees and rotting foliage, of stars twinkling in the bays of the Dubna, of the white foam collecting around the black weirs and eddying above the holes where the fish sleep on the bottom. For that reason, both my companion and I forgot to ask the woman why so much knowledge was necessary to bring people happiness. Neither of us understood.

The dawn burst forth, swathed in mist. The cloud rushed into the sky. The whole expanse of air between the cloud and the earth's horizon was filled with a pale, vast radiance. The sun's light enveloped and heated the oceans of September air above a land that was still asleep and gloomy. But within half an hour, the earth was clothed in crimson, in the russet of the reaped fields, in the damp bright green of the winter crops, in the purple of the autumn leaves and in the yellow of the birches quivering without a breeze.

'There's Suglinki!' said the woman.

The road led down towards the river, passing through the eternal black poplars which had stood there for centuries.

'Come into the cottage and have some milk to drink for the road,' said the woman. 'I haven't got a cottage of my own. I live with my friend. She's called Varvara. I've been with her all my life.'

We entered Suglinki, a neat deserted village, paved with wooden blocks. There were fuchsias in the windows, and far off the threshing machine pounded like a bass drum. The black river skirted the village in an arc.

On the threshold of the cottage, a white dog with a docked tail barked at us. 'Tuzik!' came the menacing shout of a man's voice from inside the cottage, and the dog climbed up to its place under the porch where the flattened straw was spread. Behind a partition in the cottage, someone was bustling about, perhaps getting dressed. A paper globe was hanging on a thread from the ceiling. A ginger kitten with watery eyes was playing with the globe, as if it were a football. A samovar bubbled near the stove.

'Is that you, Fenya?' enquired the voice of a young man from behind the partition. 'Mother's gone to the river to rinse the washing. We were waiting for you. We thought that Moscow had swallowed you up.'

'That's Misha, Varvara's son,' whispered Fenya. 'A captain in the artillery. He's a hero of the Soviet Union. He was badly wounded. He's just getting back on his feet.'

Fenya smiled. Her eyes were grey, but when she smiled they darkened to a gleaming blue. She took off her scarf, straightened her light brown hair and went to the cellar to fetch the milk. A tall man emerged from behind the partition wearing dark glasses and a military jacket with a high collar. He smiled in a friendly manner and introduced himself as Captain Ryabinin. On his jacket gleamed a golden star, a small star and two stripes awarded for being severely wounded. Here in the neat small cottage, this golden brilliance was quite in place, enhancing the peace of the autumn morning, the clarity of the sky, the all-encompassing silence.

When we had drunk the milk and began to make our farewells, the captain volunteered to accompany us as far as the turning in the road which would take us to Bobylin.

'Don't hold it against me,' he said, 'but I can't walk too fast. It's not my leg, you know. It's my eyes. You see, it's not long since I recovered my sight. I was badly wounded in the eyes, and it was an awfully complicated operation. I had to lie in the dark for ages, like being in a cellar. But I can see everything now. Of course, it's still a bit hazy. Anyway, let's get going.'

As we walked along the road, the captain related the story of his blindness.

'I know that you're writers,' he pursued, 'but the whole thing is just indescribable. Not because it's beyond your powers, but because I can't explain it to you clearly enough. I suppose you have to have a special talent for that sort of thing. And I don't have it.'

'How do you mean?' asked my companion. 'The complicated eye-operation?'

'No, that's another matter. It would be quite easy to explain that. But what I mean is Fenya . . . She's a remarkable woman, our Fenya. Of course she's a bit off the rails, and I suppose she ought to have done something else.'

'Well, what should she have done?' I asked.

'I don't know,' the captain hesitated. 'I can't give you an exact definition of her natural disposition. It's a bit like your profession – writing, I mean. In her case, her talents approach yours very closely. You might say they run side by side.'

'Interesting!' remarked my friend.

'Well, quite!' agreed the captain. 'What it boils down to is this. When I was in the military hospital outside Moscow, Aunt Fenya came to visit me. Well, of course she did. She's a really good-hearted person. But to look at her you would think she was a formidable woman, never ready to show pity. She's single, but she lives for others, not for herself. At that time – you can imagine – I was in a terrible state. My whole world had collapsed around me, and visual memories, as if on purpose, tormented me. I wondered if I would ever see the sun again, the water, the clouds in the sky, the faces of the people who were dear to me. Sometimes a cuckoo would screech outside the window, and I would clench my fist and swear at it. I envied the cuckoo! It was sitting on a branch and could see every grain of soil on the ground. And I was like a mole. For me the earth was like an underground dungeon. And then Fenya came. I was restless, irritable and kept on pestering her to tell me what was happening outside, around us on the earth. I was bored; she was afraid that the doctors might be cross with her and feared that her stories might make me worse. But I got round her in the end, and she started to tell me about everything. She would look out of the window and describe all that she could see. "There," she would say, "I can see a lake through the window, and there's a haze rising over it from the warmth of the sun. And in the mist I can see a little white steam-tug; from a long way off you can catch the gleam from the copper and glass. It's pulling a barge behind it loaded with birch-wood. And there's a funny little black dog running over the timber barking at the gulls. There's a small shack on the barge and in its windows you can see flower-pots with geraniums. And what magnificent blooms on those geraniums! There's a bare-footed girl in a red dress bailing out water with a pump from the hold. The water is pouring over the side, and there are little fish flying in the water as it falls. They're after the worms that were living peacefully in the hold, feeding on the dust of the birch-wood. The girl is bailing out water and singing: "Who knows and who can tell? Who knows what he's hinting at?" That barge has been over all the length and breadth of Russia, as far as Moscow itself."

'What else can you see?' I would ask Fenya.

"I can see," she would say, "the reflections of the sunbeams from the lake chasing over the ceiling of your room. They chase each other but they never meet. Your ceiling is made of pine-wood, well planed, and here and there the resin is seeping from it. When you were a little boy, I dare say you used to chew the resin of the pine."

'No,' I said, 'I chewed cherry resin.'

"The cherry resin is sweeter," said Fenya. "I'll bring you some cherry resin tomorrow."

'And she would talk to me like that for days on end. And I believed every word she said. It was so soothing to listen to her. I was even happy. It's a pity there was no one around to write down the stories she told. You could have made a book out of them. Only I've no idea what title you might have given such a book.'

' "Fenya's Stories"?' suggested my companion.

'No, they were not just stories,' the captain objected with great confidence. 'You need a more convincing title and a truer one.'

'What about "Fenya's Happiness"?'

'Still not right. It wasn't Fenya's happiness, it was mine,' the captain objected once more. 'But you're right, of course. It was Fenya's as well. She was happy to have brought me even the slightest relief.'

I recalled Fenya's saying she was uneducated, and therefore found it difficult to bring happiness to people. I told the captain of this and asked him how he would interpret what Fenya had said.

'I don't think there's any need for an interpretation,' answered the captain. 'It's quite obvious.'

'But not to us.'

'You see,' said the captain, 'everyone has his own conception of happiness. It's a personal matter. But there are some things that give rise to elation and feelings of joy in everyone.'

'Such as?'

'Take music, for example. Or magnificent buildings. I can stand for hours before a canvas of Nesterov in the Tretyakov Gallery. Fenya was talking about that kind of happiness. Only she doesn't have enough talent to pass it on to others. She would require much more knowledge.'

'In my opinion,' said my companion, 'there are times when just one talent suffices. And Fenya proved it with you.'

'Yes, you may be right,' answered the captain still unconvinced, and suddenly he smiled. 'Yes, you may very well be right,' he repeated already more convinced. 'The great pity is that Fenya's stories will go no further than Suglinki. No one else knows them.'

The captain stopped and pointed to a grey roof in a hollow in the willow-thickets.

'You see that roof,' he said, 'with the red elders beside it? That's the Bobylin mill. I may be there towards evening and I'll sit with you by the river. There are astonishing places there.'

We took our leave of the captain, and began our descent to the river through the elder-brakes. Below, the water was already sparkling, thundering by the mill, and from the village wafted the smoke of pine-wood – the smoke of a Russian autumn.

1944

Summer in Voronezh

The forest preserve by the River Usman on the outskirts
of Voronezh is the last on the border of the Don steppes.
It is cool and moans softly in the scent of the grasses,
but no sooner do you reach the edge of the wood than
your face is struck by the heat, by the harsh light; and
the steppe, distant and windy like the sea, will open
out to the ends of the earth.

Open to the view will be the windmills, which wave
their sails on barrows, kites and islands of farmstead
gardens, spread out in the distance one from another.

But above, all the sky will open up – the lofty sky of
the steppe with heaps of dark blue clouds. There are
many of them, but they hardly ever block out the sun.
Now and then the shade from them floats here and
there around the steppe. It glides so slowly that you
can walk for a long time in the shade, keeping pace
with it, sheltered from the scorching sun.

On the steppe, not far from the old lime park the
little River Kamenka gleams in the sloping ravine. It
has almost dried up; its clean, warmed water is poured
only into little pools like barrels. Over it dart aquatic
spiders, and on its banks sit sleepy frogs, breathing
heavily, hardly able to catch their breath from the dry
heat.

The lime park, dug up with trenches, destroyed and

overgrown with wild raspberries, can be heard from afar. From dawn till dusk it whistles, clicks and rings with an abundance of tits, goldfinches, robins, orioles and siskins. The hubbub of the birds never grows silent in the foliage of the limes, so tall that your head might spin just from looking up at them.

At the foot of the trees, a small, white house is hidden in the shade. Once it belonged to the almost forgotten writer, Ertel, a contemporary of Chekhov. Now in this place is a modest holiday-home.

I had my score to settle with the birds in the park. Early in the morning I would often go down to the Kamenka to fish. As soon as I walked into the park, hundreds of birds started to fuss in the branches. They were trying to hide and would shower me with dew. In panic they would fly out of the brake, as if they had surfaced from the water, and would dash headlong into the depths of the park.

It might have been a pretty spectacle, but I would get soaked with dew, and I was not very fond of that. I tried to walk quickly without making a sound, but that did not help. The more stealthily I approached some bush which was overcrowded with birds, the more intense grew their consternation, and the more plentiful was the shower of cold dew.

I would arrive at the Kamenka. The sun came up. The empty steppe gleamed with dew. There was not a soul around. Even the sharpest eye could not discern the slightest trace of human life. But no sooner had I cast my fishing-rods than a host of bare-footed boys came jumping out of the ravine.

They approached from behind in a wide arc, but so carefully that I was only conscious of their presence from their concentrated heavy breathing at my back.

The boys were silent, snorting through their noses, and without tearing themselves away looked at the red floats. From time to time, one of them scratched one of his legs with the other. From age-old experience I knew that under such circumstances the fish would stop biting. It was inexplicable, but true. It would take only one boy to stand behind my back and look over at the float for the biting to cease completely.

At first, I decided to pay the boys off, and I gave each one of them a gilded hook, but only on condition that they would go away and not get in the way of my fishing.

The boys took the hooks, thanked me in whispers and honestly went off. But within half an hour a new crowd of boys appeared, and still some way off cried out, 'Hey, mister! Give us a hook!'

I knew that I had made the worst mistake possible. I should have found a surer means of escape from the boys. Then I remembered the words of the writer, Gaidar. He had assured me that mysteries have the strongest effect upon children. So the next day when the boys crowded around me, began to snort, and the fish once more stopped biting, without turning around to look at them, I said in a sombre voice:

'You know what, kids? You can get a hundred-rouble fine for this sort of thing.'

'For what?' asked the brightest boy, with some hesitation.

'Well, just for this,' I answered.

The boys looked at each other, and without taking their eyes off me, slowly and carefully began to move backwards. They went about thirty paces in that direction, then at once turned on their heels and threw themselves helter-skelter towards the steppe. The smallest was running, stumbled and suddenly started to bawl in a deep voice. The bright boy grabbed him by the hand, gave him a smack and dragged him off behind him. The boys all disappeared.

I, no less than the boys, was amazed by what had happened. I laughed. In response behind a willow-bush someone giggled. I glanced behind the bush. There, with their faces buried in the grass and shaking with laughter, lay two tow-haired boys with long cord-whips.

'What have you stayed behind for?'

'We can't go,' said the slightly elder boy. 'We're herdsmen. Our herd's over there behind the hillock.'

'And if you hadn't got your herd with you?'

The boy got up with a grin. 'Nah!' he said. 'We wouldn't have gone anyway. We're big lads. Them? They're only tiddlers. You can fob them off with anything and they'll believe you. Now they're scared. You won't see them back for a long time.'

And that is how my friendship with the 'herdsmen', Vitya and Fedya began; and our conversations were of the most unusual nature.

'Who are you? A writer?' Fedya asked me at once.

'Yes, a writer.'

'Been writing long?'

'Quite a long time.'

'Really? That's a bit strange,' said Fedya, eyeing me suspiciously.

'Why? What's wrong?'

'Well, the fish bite, and, as I see it, you let them go.'

'You've got it wrong,' I said. 'The fish have nothing to do with it.'

'Yes they have,' remarked Fedya, offended. 'What do you mean, they've got nothing to do with it?'

At that point, the younger 'herdsman', Vitya, joined in the conversation.

'Last summer,' he piped up, choking over his words, 'a couple of other writers were fishing here. There was this bloke, Zhora, and the other one, Sasha. You should have seen that bloke, Sasha, casting his rod! The way, the way he'd haul up on his line, the way he dra–dragged it in. A perch like that! Half a yard long! One after the other. But the other bloke, Zhora. Couldn't get anything. Sat there all day long and just got a little roach, thin and feeble!'

'Shut up!' said Fedya angrily. 'You're just stupid. Don't you see? That bloke Zhora wasn't a real writer. But Sasha! There's a writer for you! He'd wrote twenty books.'

At last I understood. In Fedya's judgement, a real writer was a legendary creature, utterly talented in every domain of life; he was a master magician of his own kind with 'the golden touch'. He had to know everything, see everything, and do everything excellently.

I did not want to destroy the naïve faith of this little country herdsman. Perhaps it was because behind that naïvety there was a hidden truth, a real truth about the authentic skill of a writer. It was that truth which we often recall, but at the realization of which we do not always aim.

I felt a bit ashamed, and even in something as small as catching a fish, I swore never again to miss a bite, especially in front of Fedya. That had already become, as it were, a point of honour. Now in Moscow what I thought on the Kamenka seems a little amusing, but I could not bear the idea of Fedya saying to someone: 'That bloke, Kostya. He's not a proper writer. He can't even hook a fish. They always get away from him.'

From that time onwards, I was on my guard when I met Fedya. He wanted to know everything. He plied me with questions, but I was not able to answer all of them.

Like all herdsmen, Fedya had a vast knowledge of grasses, flowers and plants, and loved to talk about them. I also knew something about plants, but here by Voronezh there were many grasses and flowers which are not found in the more northernly regions of Russia where we live. For that reason I was very pleased that

I had brought along with me from Moscow a guide to plants.

From the steppe, from the banks of the Usman, from the forest-reserve, I brought armfuls of flowers and grasses and defined them. In that way, thanks to Fedya, I immersed myself into the tempting world of the variety of leaves, corollas, petals, stamens and ears; into the world of vegetable smells and pure colours. My room became like the dwelling of some country witch-doctor. Sheaves of dry grass hung on the walls, and the medicinal scent of the plants of the steppe clung so firmly to them that even the smell of the fading lime trees by the window could not supplant it.

And so finally came my hour of triumph.

By the banks of the Kamenka blossomed a host of fragile field-flowers. They were like tiny white stars.

One day, I walked down to the river at dawn. Fedya appeared at exactly the same time. He sat down by me, took a piece of bread from his pocket, began to chew it and to ask me about the various circumstances of life.

The sky was covered with gloom. In the grey water the bright floats stood motionless. The fish were biting poorly.

I glanced at the field-flowers at my feet and noticed that all of them were closed.

'It's going to rain,' I said to Fedya.

'How do you know?'

'By the flowers.'

I showed him the closed flowers. Fedya puckered his brow and thought for a while.

'But why do they close up before the rain?'

'So that the rain won't harm the pollen.'

I began to talk to him about the pollen, about pollination, about the way you could tell the time of day by the flowers. As I was talking, a roach bit, but I let it go.

Fedya did not even notice. He was wrapped up in my account.

'Where have you got all this from?' he asked. 'From school?'

'From books.'

'Now, if I'd known all that . . .' Fedya said slowly, and fell silent.

'What? Would you give up herding cows? Would you have gone to Voronezh?'

'No,' said Fedya, 'I belong here. I'm comfortable here. But when I get bigger, I'll be the collective farm chairman instead of Silanty Petrovich. I'll set up the seedbeds and the flowers in the village. You don't know what things I'll dream up. I'll open a bee-factory.'

A solitary raindrop fell perpendicularly on to the water and slender circles spread out. Then suddenly all around us the grass rustled and whispered; the whole stretch of water was covered with little rings, and a faint but distinct sound floated over the whirlpool. Quiet, warm rain began to fall.

Far away in the break between the soft clouds, the sun came through with wide rays, and the steppe began to steam and shine. The grass, the wheat and the earth had a stronger smell. From behind the hillock came the smell of warm milk – from the place where the herd was grazing.

'Look,' Fedya said to me. 'The grass is just like glass.'

The furry stems of the wild flowers were completely covered with raindrops, and at our feet all the plants sparkled as if they were really made of crystal.

There was nowhere for us to shelter from the rain, and we sat with Fedya's quilted jacket over our heads.

'It'll be a good summer,' said Fedya seriously.

He had probably heard these words from one of the old men in the village. The summer was really full of elusive goodness, in the light sound of the rain and in the smell of the ripening corn – the forerunner of the harvest.

1946

Nastya, the Lacemaker

During the night, from the Altau Mountains came the muffled rumbling of a storm. Frightened by the thunder, a large green cricket jumped upon the window of the military hospital and settled on the lace curtain. The wounded Lieutenant Rudnyev sat up in bed and for a long time contemplated the cricket and the curtain, on which the blue flash of the lightning revealed a complicated pattern – luxuriant rose blossoms and small crested cocks.

Morning came. The stormy, yellow sky still smoked in the window. Twin rainbows tumbled over the mountain peaks. The wet flowers of the wild peonies burnt on the window-sill like glowing embers. The atmosphere was heavy. Steam rose over the damp cliffs. On the precipice, a little river growled and thundered over the rocks.

'So this is Asia,' sighed Rudnyev. 'But it seems that the lace on the curtain is ours – northern. Some beautiful Nastya must have woven it.'

'What makes you think that?'

Rudnyev smiled. 'I've just remembered an incident,' he said, 'which happened in my unit outside Leningrad.'

He told me this story.

'In the summer of 1940, a Leningrad artist, Balashov, went to the deserted north to work and do some hunting. Balashov got off the steamer at the first village that took his fancy, and put up in the house of the local schoolmaster.

'In the same village, a young girl, Nastya, known in those parts as a lacemaker and as a beauty, lived with her father, a forest watchman. Nastya was quiet and had grey eyes like all the girls of the north.

'One day, while out hunting, Nastya's father made a careless shot and wounded Balashov in the chest. They took the wounded man back to the house of the village teacher.

'Dismayed by his bad fortune, the old man set Nastya to look after the artist. Nastya restored Balashov to health, and the pity she felt towards the wounded man gave birth to her first girlish love. But the manifestation of this love of hers was so well concealed that Balashov had not the slightest notion of it.

'Balashov had a wife in Leningrad, but he never talked about her to anyone, least of all to Nastya. All the inhabitants of the village were convinced that Balashov was single.

'As soon as his wound was healed, Balashov went back to Leningrad, but before departing he called round, uninvited, to Nastya's cottage to thank her for her care and take her some presents. Nastya accepted them.

'It was the first time that Balashov had been in the north, and he did not know the local traditions. The people of the north are very steady. They hold their ground and do not give in at once to the onslaught of new times. Balashov did not know that a man who calls round uninvited to a girl's cottage and gives her presents, if she accepts, is regarded as being betrothed to her. That's how they talk of love in the north.

'Nastya shyly asked Balashov when he would return from Leningrad to visit her in her village. Balashov, suspecting nothing, jokingly answered that he would be back very soon.

'Balashov left. Nastya waited for him. The bright summer passed by as did the damp and pungent autumn, but Balashov did not return. Nastya's joyful, impatient waiting turned to alarm, despair and shame.

'Spring brought new heartaches. It came late and lasted long. The rivers spread wide, but simply refused to come to the banks. It was not until the beginning of June that the first steamer passed by the village – without stopping.

Nastya decided to run away to Leningrad without telling her father, and to seek Balashov there. She left the village at night. Within two days she reached the railway and heard at the station that war had broken out that very morning. Over the vast, severe country the peasant girl, who never in her life had seen a train, arrived in Leningrad and sought out Balashov's flat.

'It was his wife who opened the door to Nastya – a thin woman in pyjamas, with a cigarette held in her teeth. She gazed at Nastya in amazement and told her that Balashov was not at home. He was at the Front, outside Leningrad.

'Nastya learnt the truth – Balashov was married. So he had deceived her, made fun of her love. It was awkward for Nastya to speak to Balashov's wife. She felt strange in that city flat, among the silky, dusty sofas, sprinkled powder, insistent telephone calls.

'Nastya ran away. She walked in despair through the majestic city which had been transformed into an armed military camp. She took no notice of the anti-aircraft guns on the squares, the monuments bolstered up by bags of earth, the ancient, cold gardens or the triumphal buildings.

'She walked down to the Neva. The river brought its black water up to the level of its granite embankments. She was certain that here in this water lay the only deliverance from the unbearable insult she had suffered, from love.

'Nastya took the old scarf from her head, a present from her mother, and hung it on the railings. Then she straightened her heavy tresses and placed her foot on the convoluted bars. Someone grabbed her by the hand. Nastya turned round. A thin man with floor-polishing brushes under his arm was standing behind her. His overalls were stained with yellow dye.

'The floor-polisher just shook his head and said, "What's got into you, stupid little fool, at a time like this?"

'The man, a floor-polisher called Trofimov, took Nastya home with him and entrusted her to his wife, a lift-attendant, a boisterous, hard-headed woman, who despised men.

'The Trofimovs took Nastya in. She lay ill for a long time in their garret. It was from the lift-attendant that Nastya first heard that Balashov was not to blame, that no one was obliged to know their northern customs and that only 'little idiots' like Nastya could fall blindly in love with the first man who happened to come along. The lift-attendant scolded Nastya, but she was happy. She was happy that she had not been deceived, and still hoped to see Balashov.

'It was not long before they called the floor-polisher up into the army, and the lift-attendant and Nastya were left by themselves. When Nastya recovered her health, the lift-attendant enrolled her into a course to train as a nurse. The doctors – Nastya's teachers – were impressed by her talent for tying bandages and by the nimbleness of her slender and powerful fingers. "Well, you see, I'm a lacemaker," she would answer them, almost trying to justify herself.

'The first winter of the Leningrad blockade passed by with its iron nights and gunfire. Nastya finished her training, waited to be sent to the Front, and during the nights would think of Balashov and her old father – but he, probably till the end of his life, would never understand why she had secretly run away from home. He would not scold her; he would forgive her everything. But he would never understand. It was during the spring when they finally sent Nastya to the Front outside Leningrad. Everywhere – in the smashed palace gardens, among the ruined, burnt-out buildings, in the dug-outs, in the mortar units, in the copses and in the fields – she looked for Balashov, asked after him.

'At the Front, Nastya met the floor-polisher, and this garrulous man told the soldiers from his division about the northern girl who was looking for the man she loved at the Front. Rumours about the girl grew quickly and spread like a legend. They went from division to division, from one battery to another. Despatch riders, drivers, medical orderlies, communications men, all took the rumours with them.

'The soldiers envied the unknown man whom the girl was seeking and remembered their own loved ones. In civil life, they all had sweethearts and each of them cherished their memory in their heart. When they told each other about the girl from the north, the soldiers changed the details of the story according to the powers of their imagination.

'Everyone swore that Nastya was a girl from their own native place. Ukrainians reckoned she was one of theirs; Siberians thought the same; men from Ryazan were certain that Nastya was from their town; and even the Kazakhs from the distant Asian steppe said the girl must have come to the Front from Kazakhstan.

'The tale of Nastya even reached the coastal unit where Balashov was serving. The artist, like all the other troops, was moved by the story of the unknown girl who was looking for her lover, and was impressed by the force of her love. He often thought about the girl and began to envy the man she loved. How could he have known that he was envying himself?

'Balashov's personal life had not been much of a success. He had had no joy out of his marriage. Some people are lucky! All his life he had dreamed of a great love affair, but now it was already too late to be thinking of that. His temples were turning grey . . .

'At last it turned out that Nastya found the unit in which Balashov was serving, but she did not find Balashov. He had been killed two days before and was buried in the pine forest on the shores of the gulf.'

Rudnyev fell silent.

'And then what happened?'

'And then?' Rudnyev echoed the question. 'And then our lads fought on like furies, and smashed the hell out of the German line of offence. We blew it up in the air and made it crash down to the earth like dust and mud. I've rarely seen human beings with such holy and furious anger.'

'And Nastya?'

'What about Nastya? She's giving her services to the wounded. The best sister in our part of the Front.'

1941

The Run of Time

The Moscow artist, Lavrov, was invited to paint some
Volga landscapes. Lavrov accepted the commission with
pleasure, but with his usual sluggishness it took him
all summer to get himself ready and he departed from
Moscow only at the beginning of September.

The wide-stacked steamer gleamed with its glass polished up to crystalline brilliance. The motors turned
with a low hum in the engine-room. The steamer
smoothly carried its lights and its deck, crowded with
smartly dressed passengers, past the villa groves of the
Moscow suburbs and creeks, where the chilly sunset
was already burning itself out. The woods on the banks
had already turned to russet and gold. The signal lights
of the canal shone dimly in the autumn gloom.

In spite of his advanced years, Lavrov was shy, and
found it difficult to make contact with his fellow-
passengers. He judged people most of all by their character and their paintability. Two people in particular
caught his attention on the steamer – the suntanned
girl-navigator, Sasha, and one of the passengers, a clean-
shaven old man with puffy eyelids, who was a famous
historian.

They crossed the man-made Rybinsk Sea at dawn.
Lavrov came out on to the deck which was empty and

damp with dew. Low waves ran noisily from the west to greet the turbid dawn, heralding bad weather.

The historian had also come out on to the deck. He stood on the side, turning up the collar of his overcoat, and holding down his black, old-man's hat.

Sasha ran down the steep gangway from the bridge. She was clad in a dark greatcoat, with leather gloves and a beret, under which she had bunched up her chestnut hair. Sasha had just changed over from the night-watch. Her face was ruddy from the cold and her lips were chapped.

'Hello!' she said cheerily to Lavrov, and smiled at him. 'Do you admire the sea?'

'Rather!' answered Lavrov. 'It's almost impossible to believe that all this was made by human hands.'

'I come from these parts myself – from Mologa,' answered Sasha. 'When I was a girl, right here at the bottom of the sea,' she pointed to the waves flying in the pink light of the dawn, 'I used to pick mushrooms. Not so long ago. This sea is younger than I am.'

'The momentum of events has taken such a swift turn that history is quite unable to keep abreast of them,' said the historian, pulling his hat down almost as far as his ears. 'Events move on traversing and running ahead of our laborious chain of thought. One would require a whole army of historians to establish this flight of time in our scientific researches.'

Near Kineshma the steamer overtook a string of rafts.

The gusty wind carried along the light, broken clouds. Their shadows scudded over the river and the wooded banks which approached the water with sandy scree. Following the shadow, the sun kept breaking through, and at once everything around began to sparkle with a host of colours and reflections. A flock of river gulls would now fly out from the shadow, flaring up with snowy whiteness, and once again hurtle off into the shade; here a red flag would blaze up over an isolated hut on the shore, no doubt the Selsovet, the village 'Soviet of Peoples' Deputies'; there the pine forest would be all of a quiver and glitter as if it had been drenched with slanting, gleaming rain; then all at once the forest would be draped in a green, gloomy shroud, and its protracted, majestic sound would fly towards the steamer.

The waves churned up by the steamer splashed the rafts. On thick pine-logs, bound together by steel hawsers, stood girls with boat-hooks, shouting something, but the wind carried their voices away to the other side and it was impossible to make out what they were calling. Only their firm white teeth were visible on their suntanned, laughing faces, their head-scarves of many colours and the calico hems of their skirts flapping on their dark-skinned legs.

Sasha was standing on the bridge. She put a brass megaphone to her lips and shouted, 'How's it going, girls?'

'All right, Sasha,' the girls shouted back the answer in unison, waving their scarves.

'Are you floating far?'

'Right up to Stalingrad! Goodby–ye! Don't forget us! Don't forget the Volga girls.'

Looking at the girls, Lavrov realized that for them Sasha was one of their own, that this woman-navigator was probably well known and loved on the Volga. Of course it could not have been otherwise. It is not often that you find women navigating the Volga.

That evening, Lavrov complained to Sasha that he thought that these young raft-girls, on a windy day of changing colour, would have made a wonderful subject for a picture, but he had not even had the chance to make a sketch. Everything rushed by so quickly.

'You might have held the steamer back for a moment,' Lavrov told Sasha jokingly.

'I understand very well,' answered Sasha, 'but, Vladimir Petrovich, that is strictly forbidden.'

'Ah, you people! You're like machines. You underestimate the meaning of beauty in our life!'

'Oh no!' Sasha hotly objected. 'We love and prize beauty very much. But you try to understand us as well.'

'What in particular do I have to understand?'

'Well, just imagine all the complications in the coordination of transport over such a large country,' answered Sasha. 'The movement of all the trains, steamers and aeroplanes; the network of intersection points on their journeys, where they all have to be according to a timetable. All that is necessary to make life run smoothly without hitches. Don't you call that beauty?'

'Yes, perhaps,' agreed Lavrov. 'I hadn't thought of that.'

They were going down the Volga. The gilded hills stretched out on the steep, straight banks. The steel masts of the electricity transmitters stood knee-deep in the autumn foliage. On the top through the taut wires the electric current flowed unremittingly. For some reason, Lavrov imagined that the current reflected the colour blue. Perhaps because whenever the current manifested itself, it always gave off blue flashes.

The left bank went off into the mist, which was full of different hues – pink, gold, blue, lilac, purple and bronze, wide and washed-out splashes of colour. Lavrov knew that these were the woods and clouds lit by the evening sun, which are visible through the mist, precipices on the banks and, perhaps, far-off white buildings of towns invisible in the gloom.

One day, Lavrov was sitting on a bench on the upper deck near the captain's bridge where there were no passengers. On the trestle, he had set his frame before him, and with quick, wide strokes he sketched on his canvas a world that grew silent towards the evening of air, mist, multicoloured water, reflections and distances that were turning to gold.

Sasha was keeping her watch on the bridge. Several times, she threw a questioning glance at Lavroc, then looked up at the sky. She was vexed that the evening was approaching so quickly, and that very soon all that brilliance would disappear and dusk would colour everything in a monotone, grey light. 'He'll not make it,' thought Sasha. 'He should really paint a bit faster.'

She tugged the string of the siren. The steamer cried out with a protracted warning hoot. A boat was crossing its bows. The steamer was heading quickly towards it, and Lavrov suddenly saw: on the boat stood a young woman with her jacket unbuttoned. She was clutching to herself an armful of autumn twigs and was looking towards the steamer. At the oars sat a young man burnt black by the sun. He stopped rowing and also looked at the steamer. The reflection of the branches played on the water at the side of the boat.

That whole evening, the woman, the cloud, radiant over the river like a cluster of grapes – all struck Lavrov as such a clear embodiment of the peace and silence of this country which was his own and so extraordinary, that he merely sighed and looked angrily at Sasha. Lifting his brush, he waited for a brief moment, hoping that Sasha might stop the steamer just for a minute, but her face was stony, even malicious.

The boat carrying the woman sailed off quickly, rocking from side to side, into the dusk. The last glow of the sunset fell on to the armful of autumn twigs. The darkness was unable to extinguish completely the golden light on the leaves.

Lavrov angrily banged his paint-box shut and went off to his cabin. Passing by the bridge, he looked obliquely at Sasha, who blushed and turned her face away.

'Very well!' thought Lavrov. 'We'll have to talk about this!'

In his cabin, he considered for a long time what he might say to Sasha. He worked out a whole speech of indictment. But that evening he did not see her. Perhaps she had gone to sleep straight after her watch, and overnight his prepared accusation somehow lost its bloom and even seemed to him a bit silly.

Lavrov thought hard: 'What did he want? The whole of life to stop just for him? But that would never happen. It will always continue in a wide and multicoloured stream towards the distance we call our future. If you lag behind, the stream grows dim and fades from your sight, and you will never catch it up.

'The girl's right, I suppose,' Lavrov finally decided. 'I really shouldn't have been angry with her.' The next day when Lavrov met Sasha on the deck, Lavrov just looked at her grey, shyly smiling eyes, and said, 'I'll certainly paint you. But not now. In the winter in Moscow. Are we agreed?'

'Very well,' answered Sasha. 'Thank you, Vladimir Petrovich.'

She laid her light, trusting hand on Lavrov's sleeve.

He glanced at the river. The lines of lights shone, playing in the autumn darkness. Fresh and humid, with black, gigantic, almost glassy billows, the Volga in all its breadth rolled towards the chasm of the night; stretching out to the stripes of light and breaking them up, it took with it the reflection of the lamps. The steamer was heading towards the Kuibyshev dam, which was being constructed.

In December Sasha came to Moscow for the annual exhibition of paintings in the Tretyakov Gallery.

It was evening. The snow was falling lazily, and as one looked up from the street into the well-lit windows of the houses, it seemed as if there, in those houses, thousands of candles were burning, and some quiet winter festival was taking place in them.

There were not many people in the exhibition. Sasha quickly walked through the halls, searching for Lavrov's picture. From afar she caught sight of it, stopped, and for a moment of anxiety she found it hard to catch her breath.

How, with what incomprehensible power, had that taciturn, even *gauche*-looking man captured for all time that amazing evening on the river? How had he seen in it more charms and colours than she had seen at exactly the same moment? In what did his power reside? In his talent? Or in the joining of talent with love for his amazing country?

'How could he have painted from memory that evening, the boat, the woman with the armful of twigs?' Sasha asked herself. 'I didn't even hold the steamer back, though I knew very well that he wanted me to.'

The longer Sasha looked at the picture, the stronger grew her desire to thank Lakrov, and even perhaps with tenderness and surprise to touch lightly his thin hand, stained with paint.

Sasha stood and looked at the painting from far off, and her anxiety changed to an unexpected, impetuous joy. 'How fine everything is!' she thought. 'Even this fluffy, lazy, face-tickling evening snow outside the windows.

'Everything! Everything!'

1951

Hot Bread

As the cavalry was passing through Berezhki, a German shell exploded on the boundary of the village and wounded one of the black horses in the leg. The commander abandoned the lame horse in the village, and the detachment proceeded, raising the dust and jangling the bridles, traversing groves and hills, where the wind ruffled the golden rye.

The horse was adopted by the miller, Pankrat. The mill had been idle for ages, but the dust of the flour over the ages had for ever eaten into Pankrat. It lay like a grey crust on his quilted jacket and cap. From beneath his cap the miller's sharp eyes surveyed all. Pankrat was an irrascible old man, quick and ready for work, and the children said he was a wizard.

Pankrat cured the horse. The horse became attached to the mill and patiently carried clay, manure and sticks, helping Pankrat to clean the dyke.

It was hard for Pankrat to feed the horse sufficiently, and the horse started to go begging from house to house. He would stop, snort, knock on the gate with his muzzle, and they would bring out for him beetroot tops or stale bread, and sometimes he even got sweet carrots. The people of the village said that the horse belonged to no one, he was really common property, and everyone considered it his duty to give him food. And apart from that, the horse was wounded; he had suffered at the hands of the enemy.

In Berezhki was a boy who lived with his grandmother. His real name was Filka, but his nickname was 'Hop it!'. Filka was a sullen, distrustful boy, and his favourite expression was 'Hop it!'. If the boy next door asked him to come out on his stilts, or to go and look for some spent cartridges, Filka would growl angrily: 'Hop it! Go and look yourself.' When his grandmother told him about his bad manners, Filka would turn on her and mutter: 'Hop it! You make me fed up.'

That year, the winter had been warm. The smoke hung in the air. No sooner had the snow fallen than it melted. The wet crows sat on the stove-pipes to dry their feathers, jostling and cawing at one another. The water had not frozen by the mill-race, but stood black and still, and little pieces of ice floated on top of it.

By that time, Pankrat had repainted the mill and was getting ready to grind the wheat. The village wives complained that they were getting short measure. The flour only lasted two or three days and the rest of the grain just lay there, unground.

On one of those warm, grey days, the wounded horse put its nose on the gate of Filka's grandmother's house. The old lady was not at home, and Filka was sitting at the table, chewing a slice of bread thickly sprinkled with salt.

Filka got up unwillingly and went out to the gate. The horse shifted from foot to foot, stretching its neck out for some bread. 'Hop it, you devil!' cried Filka, landing the horse a hefty blow on the lips. The horse drew back, shook its head, and Filka hurled the bread far away on to the crumbly snow and shouted, 'Beggars are never satisfied. There take your bread. Go and dig it out of the snow with your muzzle. Go on! Dig!'

And then, after that wicked outburst, there came about in Berezhki such extraordinary events that even today people talk of them, wagging their heads, because they do not even know themselves whether they happened or not.

A tear fell from the horse's eye. The horse neighed long and pitifully, swished its tail, and at once a piercing wind howled down the chimney-pipes and whistled through the bare trees, over the fences and in the stoves; the powdery snow blew on Filka's face almost choking him. Filka hurried back to the porch as the storm swept around him and lashed against his eyes, but he could not find the porch. Wisps of frozen straw from the thatch flew in the wind, the starling-boxes broke into pieces and the torn-off shutters clattered. And columns of snow dust rose higher and higher from the neighbouring fields and approaching the village, crackling, whirring, chasing one another.

Filka rushed into the cottage at last, pressed himself against the door and exclaimed: 'Hop it!' He listened intently. The wind snowstorm raged, but through its howling Filka heard a soft, brief swishing, like the swishing of a horse's tail when the animal is angry and strikes at its own flanks.

The storm began to abate towards evening, and only then was Filka's grandmother able to get back to the cottage from the neighbouring house. By night the sky became pale green like ice, the stars froze in the heavenly vault, and the prickly frost settled over the village. No one saw it, but everyone heard the crunch of its felt boots over the hard snow and heard how the frost mischievously squeezed the thick logs in the walls, making them crack and split.

The grandmother was crying and told Filka that the wells had surely frozen over, and now certain death awaited them. There was no water and everyone's flow had been used up. The mill could no longer work because the river had suddenly frozen to the very bottom.

Filka also cried from fear when the mice began to run out from under the floorboards and hide themselves in the straw under the stove, where there was still a little warmth left. 'Hop it! Horrible things!' he shouted at the mice, but the mice still crawled out of the floorboards. Filka climbed on to the stove, wrapped himself in a sheepskin and, shivering, listened to his grandmother's wailing.

'A hundred years ago,' she said, 'we had a frost as harsh as this in our neighbourhood. It froze the wells and killed the birds; it wasted the woods and the gardens to the very roots. The seeds withered and died in the ground. It was ten years before the trees blossomed and the grass grew after that. Our land was bare. All the animals ran past fearing that the place had become a desert.'

'But why did the frost come?' asked Filka.

'Because of the wickedness of men,' said the old lady. 'An old soldier was passing through our village and begged some bread from one of the cottages. But the master was an evil man. He felt tired and in a mood for bawling, and gave the old man only a stale crust. But he did not give it to him in his hands but just threw it on to the ground, saying: "There you are! Chew that!" "I can't pick up the bread from the ground," replied the old soldier. "I have a wooden leg." "And what did you do with your leg?" asked the peasant. "I lost it in the Balkan hills when we were fighting against the Turks," answered the soldier. "Well, if you're as hungry as all that," laughed the peasant, "you'll pick it up. There are no servants around here to wait on you." The soldier groaned, somehow managed to pick up the crust, and saw that the bread was covered in green mould. Poison! The soldier went into the yard and whistled, and at once a snowstorm blew up. The whole village was surrounded by a whirling blizzard, and the roofs of the houses were torn off. Afterwards a cruel frost set in. Then the peasant died.'

'What did he die of?' asked Filka hoarsely.

'Of the coldness of his heart,' said the old lady.

She was silent for a while, then added, 'You know, at this time as well some bad offender might have come to live in Berezhki who had already done something wicked. That's why the frost has come.'

'But what's to be done now, old woman?' asked Filka, from under his sheepskin. 'Are we all to die?'

'Why should we die? We must hope.'

'For what?'

'We must hope that the bad person makes amends for his evil deed.'

'But how to make amends?' sobbed Filka.

'Pankrat, the miller knows about that. He is a clever, wise old man. You'll have to ask him. But you will not be able to get to the mill in this frost, will you? Your blood will freeze.'

'Let him hop it! Old Pankrat!' said Filka and remained silent. But during the night, he crept from the stove. His grandmother was sitting asleep on the bench. Behind the windows, the air was dark blue, thick and terrible. In the clear sky above the black poplars stood the full moon, attired like a bride with a pink crown.

Filka, wrapped in his sheepskin, dashed into the street and ran towards the mill. The snow sang under his feet like a happy band of woodcutters sawing at the roots of the birch trees in the grove by the river. It seemed that even the air was frozen, and between the earth and the moon there was a great void, burning and so clear, that even if a speck of dust had risen a mile away from the earth, it would have been visible and would have shone and twinkled like a little star.

The black willows by the millstream were becoming grey with frost. Their branches glistened like crystal.

The air pricked Filka's breast. He could no longer run, but walked heavily, raking up the snow with his boots.

Filka knocked at the window of Pankrat's cottage, and as he did so the wounded horse in the shed behind neighed and banged its hooves. Filka moaned, squatted down in fright and tried to hide himself. Pankrat opened the door, took Filka by the scruff of the neck and dragged him inside the cottage.

'Sit down by the stove,' he said. 'Tell me what you've come for before you freeze.'

Filka, weeping, told Pankrat how he had offended the wounded horse and how because of what he had done the frost had come down on the village.

'Ah well!' sighed Pankrat. 'That is bad indeed. It turns out that we are all suffering because of you. Why did you offend the horse? For what reason? You are a thoughtless citizen!'

Filka snorted and wiped away his tears with his sleeve.

'Now stop your howling!' ordered Pankrat strictly. 'You're all very good at howling. You got up to mischief – and now you blabber. I don't see the point of it. My mill has stopped as if it has been choked by the frost for ages. There's no flour; there's no water; and I have no idea what to suggest.'

'What can I do now, Grandfather Pankrat?' asked Filka.

'You'll have to find a way to rescue us all from the frost. Then you will not stand guilty in the eyes of the people. And in the eyes of the wounded horse you will become a pure and cheerful person. Everyone will pat you on the shoulder and forgive you. Do you understand?'

'I do,' answered Filka in a low voice.

'Well, find a way out then. I'll give you an hour and a quarter.'

In Pankrat's hall there lived a magpie. She couldn't

sleep for the cold, and perched on a horse collar, over-
hearing all that was being said. Then, turning her head
and looking around, she hopped to a crack in the door.
She scurried outside, jumped on to the railings and
flew straight to the south. The magpie was old and
experienced and purposefully flew close to the ground,
because the trees in the woods gave off some warmth,
and so the magpie was not afraid of freezing. No one
saw her. Only a fox in the aspen bank put its muzzle
out of its lair and sniffed around. The fox noticed how,
like a dark shadow, the magpie rushed along the sky,
then he shied back into his lair and sat for a long time
scratching and wondering where on earth the magpie
could be off to on such an awful night.

All this time, Filka was sitting on a bench, fidgeting
and thinking.

'Well?' said Pankrat at last, rolling his rough cigar.
'Your time's up. Out with it! You won't have a minute's
grace.'

'Grandfather Pankrat,' said Filka. 'As soon as it is
light, I'll round up the children in the village. We'll take
crowbars, shovels and axes, and we'll go on breaking the
ice in the mill-race until we get down to the water and
the wheel starts turning. As soon as the water starts to
flow, release the mill. Turn the wheel twenty times; it
will warm up and begin to grind. Then, you see, there
will be water and flour, and everyone will be saved,'

'Huh! You're a clever fellow,' said the miller. 'I know
there's water under the ice, but if the ice is as thick as
you are tall, then what will you do?'

'Hop it!' said Filka. 'We children will break it no
matter how thick it is.'

'And if you get cold?'

'We'll light bonfires.'

'And if the other children won't agree to pay for your
stupidity with the sweat of their brow? If *they* say, "Let

him hop it; it's his own fault. Let him chop the ice up himself"?'

'They'll agree! I'll plead with them. Our children are good.'

'Well. Get on with it. Get your children together, and I'll have a word with the old men. Perhaps even they will put on their mittens and apply themselves to the crowbars.'

On frosty days the sun comes up crimson, bathed in heavy smoke. And that morning such a sun rose over Berezhki. The regular striking of the crowbars could be heard over the river. There was a crackle of bonfires and children and old men worked from early dawn breaking up the ice by the mill. And in the excitement, no one noticed how after midday the sky was strewn with low clouds and a constant warm breeze blew through the grey-flecked willows. And when they did notice that the weather had changed, the willow branches were already thawing and the wet birch grove over the river resounded joyfully.

The wind was blowing from the south, and with every passing hour it became warmer and warmer. The icicles on the roofs dropped and broke with a crack. The crows flew from under the eaves, and once more dried themselves on the stove-pipes, jostling and cawing.

Only the old magpie was missing. She flew home towards the evening when the ice began to subside in the warmth; at the mill the work proceeded quickly and the first unfrozen patch of dark water appeared.

The boys threw off their flapped hats and cheered. Pankrat declared that if there had not been a warm breeze, then, whatever you said, the children and the old men would not have been able to chop the ice. And the magpie sat on the brittle-willow over the dyke, jabbering and wagging her tail. She bowed on all sides telling her story, but no one but the crows understood a word she said. The magpie related that she had flown south as far as the warm sea, where the summer wind slept in the mountains. She had woken him up, chattered to him about the cruel frost, and had asked him to help the people and drive the frost away.

The wind would not have refused *her* – not the magpie – and he started to blow, flying over the fields, whistling and chuckling at the frost. And if you listen very carefully you can still hear how the warm water in the ravines bubbles and seethes under the snow, washing the roots of the whortleberry, breaking the ice on the river.

Everyone knows that the magpie is the most talkative bird in the world and for that reason the crows did not believe her. They just cawed amongst themselves and thought that the old lady was lying again. To this day, no one know whether the magpie was telling the truth or whether she had made it all up just to boast. The only thing we do know is that by evening the ice cracked, broke apart, the children and the old men pressed it down and water gushed with a roar into the mill-race.

The old wheel began to creak, the icicles showered down from it, and slowly it began to turn. The millstones ground together and the wheel turned quicker and quicker. Suddenly the whole mill shuddered, rocked violently and started to knock, wheeze and crush the grain.

Pankrat poured out the corn and warm flour flowed from the millstones into the sacks. The women dipped their frozen hands into it and laughed. In every yard rang out the sound of birch being chopped for firewood. The cottages were aglow with fire in the burning stoves. The women kneaded the thick, sweet dough, and anything alive in the cottages – children, cats and even the mice – thronged around them, but the women slapped the children on the back with their hands, which were white with flour, to stop them crawling into the trough itself and getting in the way of the work.

By nightfall in the village there was such a good smell of hot bread with its golden crust, and cabbage-leaves burnt to the bottom, that even the foxes crept out of their holes and sat on the snow, whimpering softly and considering how they might snatch a small piece of the bread from the people.

The next morning, Filka came with the other children to the mill. The wind chased the whispy clouds over the blue sky, not allowing them a moment's pause for breath. For this reason, the ground was covered alternately with cold shade and sometimes with warm sunny patches.

Filka took a loaf of fresh bread, and the smallest of all the boys, Nikolai, held a carved wooden cellar of rough, yellow salt. Pankrat came out on to the door-step and said: 'What's all this then? Bringing me bread and salt?[12] What do I deserve this for?'

'No!' cried the children. 'You will have something else. But this is for the wounded horse. It's from Filka. We want them to be friends again.'

'Well,' said Pankrat, 'it's not only people who need an apology. Hang on a moment and I'll bring the horse round.'

Pankrat opened the doors of the stable and led out the horse. The horse came out, stretched his head forward, neighed and caught the smell of the fresh bread. Filka broke the loaf, salted it from the cellar and tendered it to the horse. But he would not take the bread and shifted from one leg to another, then moved backwards into the shed. He was afraid of Filka. Then Filka wept loudly before the whole village. The children whispered together and fell silent, but Pankrat patted the horse on the neck and said, 'Don't be afraid, old fellow! Filka's not a wicked person. Why do you offend him? Take the bread and make friends.'

The horse shook his head, pondered a while, then cautiously stretched out his neck and finally took the bread from Filka's hands with his soft lips. He ate one piece, sniffed at Filka and took a second piece. Filka grinned through his tears; the horse chewed the bread and snorted. When he had eaten all the bread, he laid his head on Filka's shoulder, sighed and closed his eyes, feeling full and happy.

Everyone smiled and rejoiced. Only the old magpie sat on the brittle-willow and chattered angrily. She might have been boasting again that she was the only one who had made the horse and Filka friends again. But no one listened to her and no one understood. And the magpie got all the more angry and rattled away like a machine-gun.

The Ring of Steel

Grandfather Kuzma lived with his little granddaughter, Varyusha, in the village of Mokhovoe, on the very edge of the forest.

The winter had been harsh with a piercing wind and had brought heavy snow. The temperature had not risen once throughout the whole winter and not a drop of bustling water had melted on the plank roof of the cottage. At night, in the wood, the wolves, frozen to the marrow, would howl. Grandfather Kuzma said that they were howling because they envied the people; even a wolf would like to live in a cottage, scratching itself as it lay by the stove, warming its frozen, shaggy coat.

Half-way through the winter, the old man's tobacco ran out. He coughed violently, complained about his poor health and said that if he could only have a puff or two he would feel better.

One Sunday, Varyusha went to the neighbouring village of Perebory to buy some tobacco for her grandfather. The railway line passed right by the village. Varyusha bought the tobacco, tucked it into her calico bag and walked to the station to look at the trains. It was not very often that they stopped in the village of Perebory. They almost always passed by with a clank and a rattle.

There were two soldiers sitting on the platform. One

of them had a beard and bright, grey eyes. There came the whistle of a steam-engine. They could already see it in a cloud of smoke, furiously rushing towards the station from the distant black forest.

'The express,' said the soldier with the beard. 'Look out, little girl! The train will blow you away and you'll fly up to the sky.'

The engine swept through the station. The snow whirled round and stuck on their eyes. Then came the clanking of the wheels, answering and chasing each other. Varyusha held tightly on to the signal pole and closed her eyes, as if she might really be lifted up from the ground and whisked away by the train.

When the train had gone through and the powdery snow, whirling through the air, had settled down, the soldier with the beard asked Varyusha, 'What's that you've got in your bag? Not tobacco, is it?'

'Yes, tobacco,' answered Varyusha.

'Can you sell me some? I'd love a smoke.'

'My grandfather, Kuzma, wouldn't let me sell it,' answered Varyusha strictly. 'He needs it for his cough.'

'Oh, I see,' said the soldier, 'my little flower petal in felt boots! What a serious one you are!'

'But you can take as much as you need,' said Varyusha, offering the soldier her bag. 'Go on. Have a smoke.'

The soldier sprinkled a good handful of tobacco into his greatcoat pocket, rolled a fat cigarette, had a puff, and taking Varyusha under the chin looked into her blue eyes and smiled. 'What a one you are!' he repeated. 'A little pansy with plaits! Now what can I give you in return? Perhaps this?'

Out of his pocket the soldier pulled a little ring made of steel, blew the bits of tobacco and salt from it, rubbed it on the sleeve of his coat and put it on Varyusha's finger.

'Wear it for good health. This ring is really magic. See how it shines.'

'But why is it magic?' asked Varyusha, blushing.

'Because,' said the soldier, 'if you wear it on your middle finger it will bring good health to you and your grandfather, Kuzma. If you wear it on this one, on your ring-finger' – the soldier pulled out Varyusha's frozen, red finger – 'you'll have great joy. Supposing, for instance, you want to see the whole world with all its wonders, all you have to do is put the ring on your index-finger, and lo and behold! you'll see it.'

'Shall I?' asked Varyusha.

'Oh, you believe him,' droned the other soldier from under the upturned collar of his greatcoat. 'He's a wizard. Have you ever heard that word?'

'Yes. I have.'

'That's it!' laughed the soldier. 'He's an old sapper. He hasn't ever been touched by a mine yet.'

'Thank you,' said Varyusha, and ran off home to Mokhovoe.

There was a biting wind and the snow was falling thickly. Varyusha kept touching the ring, turning it round and round on her finger and looking to see how it shone in the winter glow.

'But the soldier forgot to tell me what happens if you put it on your little finger. I wonder what happens then? Let me try it on my little finger and see.'

She slid it on to her little finger, but the finger was too small and the ring would not stay there. It fell on to the thick snow by the path and at once disappeared into the deep, white ground.

Varyusha groaned and started to dig up the snow with her hands. But the ring was not to be found. Her fingers turned blue, and became so numb with the frost that she could not bend them any more.

Varyusha started to cry. She had lost her ring! Now Grandfather Kuzma would never get well and she would never find the greatest joy, nor would she see the whole world with all its wonders. In the place she had dropped the ring, Varyusha stuck an old fir branch in the snow and walked home. She wiped away her tears with her mittens, but they still kept flowing and froze on her face, and because of that her eyes pricked and hurt.

Grandfather Kuzma was delighted with the tobacco and made the whole cottage full of smoke. About the ring he said: 'Don't be sad, silly girl. It'll turn up where you lost it. Ask Sidor. He'll find it for you.'

There was an old sparrow, called Sidor, who slept on a pole, puffed up like a ball. Sidor lived in Kuzma's cottage the whole winter, pleasing himself as if he were the owner. He had such a character that it was not only Varyusha whom he made reckon with him, but Grandfather Kuzma as well. He'd gobble up the pudding straight out of the basin and would try to snatch the bread from their hands, and if anyone chased him away, he would get offended, fly into a temper, and would fight and chirp so angrily that the neighbouring sparrows would fly up to the eaves and listen to him intently. And then they would noisily scold him for his silly manners, telling him that he lived in a cottage, warm and well fed, and that was still not enough for him.

The next day Varyusha got hold of Sidor, wrapped him up in her scarf and took him to the forest. Only the tip of the fir branch was sticking out of the snow. Varyusha sat the sparrow on the top of the branch and said, 'You have a look and rummage for it. Perhaps you'll find it.'

But Sidor cocked his eye, looked doubtfully at the snow and chirped, 'Now, how d'you like that? Making a fool of me! Off with you, off with you!' he repeated, tore himself from the branch and flew back to the cottage.

And the ring was never found.

Grandfather Kuzma's cough became worse.

Before the spring came, he hobbled to the stove. He

hardly left his place and kept asking for something to drink. Varyusha brought him cold water in an iron jug.

The snow swirled over the village and covered the cottages. The pine trees were bowed by the weight of the snow and Varyusha could no longer recognize the place in the forest where she had dropped the ring. She would sit hiding behind the stove, softly weeping out of pity for her grandfather and scolding herself. 'Stupid girl!' she whispered. 'You've been naughty and you dropped the ring. And this is what you've got in return. This is what you deserve.'

She hit herself with her fists on the top of her head to punish herself, and Grandfather Kuzma asked, 'Why are you making such a noise? Who are you shouting at?'

'At Sidor,' Varyusha answered. 'He's become so disobedient. He's always trying to pick a fight.'

One morning, Varyusha was woken by Sidor who had jumped on to the window-frame and was knocking on the pane with his beak. Varyusha opened and screwed up her eyes. Chasing one another, long drops of water were falling from the roof. The hot light hit the little window. The jackdaws cawed.

Varyusha glanced at the street. A warm breeze blew into her eyes and ruffled her hair.

'The spring has come!' said Varyusha.

The black twigs glistened, the wet, crackling snow climbed down from the roof, and beyond the village boundary the damp wood stirred with an air of importance and joy. The spring came over the field like a young mistress. She only had to glance at a ravine when at once the brook came running through and began to gurgle and sing harmoniously. The spring came on and the sound of the streams became louder and louder with each of her steps.

In the wood, the snow grew darker. At first the brown conifer needles were revealed, which had been scattered upon it during the winter; then the hundreds of dry twigs which the December storms had broken off; and then it was stained yellow by the dead leaves of the previous year; the thawed patches of earth were slowly uncovered and at the edge of the last snowdrifts the first flowers of the coltsfoot began to appear.

Varyusha found the old fir branch in the wood – the very same branch that she had stuck in the snow where she had dropped the ring – and she carefully began to scatter the old leaves and the empty fir-cones thrown around by the woodpeckers and to remove the twigs and the rotten moss. Under one of the black leaves something glittered. Varyusha sat down with a cry of joy. There it was – the steel ring! It was not even rusty.

Varyusha grasped it, put it on her middle finger and rushed off home.

As she was running to the cottage, still far off, she caught sight of Grandfather Kuzma. He had come out of the cottage and, as he sat on the earth-bunker, his blue tobacco smoke wafted over him to the sky. It was as if Kuzma were sunning himself in the spring air and steam was spiralling over him.

'There you are,' said the grandfather. 'There you are, you silly girl. You rushed out of the cottage and forgot to close the door. The spring air freshened the whole cottage, and at once my illness went away. I'll just have my smoke, then I'll get my chopper; I'll gather some firewood, light the stove and bake some rye-cakes.'

Varyusha laughed, stroked her grandfather's shaggy grey hair, and cried, 'Thank the ring, Grandfather Kuzma! It's made you better.'

All day long, she wore the ring on her middle finger in order to chase away her grandfather's illness more quickly. Only in the evening, as Varyusha was getting ready to go to sleep, did she take it off and put it on to her ring-finger. With that the greatest joy should have come, but it was tardy and would not come. Still waiting for it, Varyusha fell asleep.

She got up early, put on her clothes and went out of the cottage. The still warm dawn was creeping over the earth; the stars were still twinkling on the edge of the sky. Varyusha went to the forest and stopped at the edge of it. There was something ringing, as if someone were carefully turning the bells in a spire. What could it be?

Varyusha bent down, listened carefully and clasped her hands together. The white snowdrops were swinging to greet the dawn and every flower called out, as if there was a little grasshopper beetle sitting in it, hitting a silvery spider's web with its foot. On the top of a fir tree a woodpecker beat five times.

'Five o'clock!' thought Varyusha. 'So early! And be quiet!'

Suddenly, high up in the branches an oriole sang out in the golden light of the dawn. Varyusha stood there, her mouth half open, listening, smiling. She was embraced by the strong, warm, kindly wind, and something rustled by her. The hazel trembled, and yellow powder scattered from the nut-catkins. Someone unseen passed by Varyusha, carefully separating the twigs. A cuckoo called and bowed to the stranger as he passed.

'Who on earth can that be,' thought Varyusha, 'that I didn't recognize him?'

She did not know that before her passed Spring. She laughed loudly; her laughter rang out over the whole forest as she ran homewards. The greatest joy, the joy you cannot hold in your hands, sang in her heart.

The spring flared up and grew happier with every passing day. Such light poured from the sky that Grandfather Kuzma's eyes became as narrow as chinks but kept smiling.

Then over the woods, over the water-meadows, over

the gullies as if someone had sprinkled them with magic water, thousands and thousands of different coloured flowers burst into bloom.

Varyusha thought that she might slip the ring on to her index-finger to see the whole world with all its wonders, but when she gazed at all these flowers, the sticky birch leaves, the clear sky and the warm sun; when she heard the crowing of the cocks, the sound of the water and the whistling of the birds over the fields, she did not put the band on her index-finger.

'I'll manage,' she thought. 'Nowhere in this wide world can it be so good as it is in our Mokhovoe. This is real bliss! It's quite right, you know, what Grandfather Kuzma says. Our land is true Paradise and there's nowhere better on the whole earth!'

1946

The Adventures of a
Rhinocerous Beetle

(A Soldier's Tale)

When Pyotr Terentyev was leaving the village for the war, his little son, Styopa, couldn't think of anything to give his father as a keepsake; finally he made him a present of an old rhinocerous beetle. He had caught it in the kitchen-garden and put it in a matchbox. The beetle was upset and knocked, demanding to be set free. But Styopa would not let him out, and slid in a few blades of grass so that the beetle would not die of hunger. The rhinocerous beetle chewed at the grass, but still continued to knock and make a fuss.

Styopa cut a little window in the matchbox to make sure that there would be a fresh supply of air. The beetle poked his hairy claw out of the window and tried to catch hold of Styopa's finger. He probably wanted to scratch him out of spite. But Styopa would not let him have his finger. In desperation, the beetle started to buzz so much that Akulina, Styopa's mother, cried out, 'Let the horrible thing go. It buzzes and buzzes all day long. It's making my head ache'.

Pyotr Terentyev smiled when he saw his son's pres-

ent. He ruffled Styopa's hair with his rough hand and
hid the box with the beetle in it in his gas-mask case.

'Only make sure you don't lose him. Look after him,'
said Styopa.

'Such fine gifts must not be lost,' replied Pyotr. 'I'll
look after him somehow.'

Either the beetle liked the smell of rubber, or perhaps
he found the scent of the greatcoat and black bread
pleasant. Anyway, the beetle calmed down and followed
Pyotr right up to the Front.

At the Front, the soldiers were fascinated by the
beetle. They fingered its stiff horn, and when they heard
Pyotr's story about his son's present, they exclaimed:
'So the little fellow even thought of that. But your
beetle's a real soldier. We'll give him the rank of lance-
corporal – not bad for a beetle.'

The soldiers were interested to know how long the
beetle could live and what sort of food it needed. They
wondered what Pyotr was going to give him to eat
and drink. Because even a beetle cannot exist without
water.

Pyotr laughed shyly and told them that an ear of corn
would last him a week. Beetles don't need that much.

One night, Pyotr was dozing in the trench and
dropped the box with the beetle in it out of his bag. For
a long time, the beetle moved around, bored a hole in
the box, crawled out, twirled his whiskers, and listened
intently. Far away the earth was thundering and there
were flashes of yellow lightning.

The beetle climbed on to an elder bush at the side of
the trench to get a better view. He had never seen such
a storm. There was far too much lightning, and the
stars did not seem to be fixed in the sky, as they did in
the beetle's homeland in Pyotr's village, but shot up
from the earth; they burst into a dazzling light, turned
smoky and went out. The thunder rumbled on
incessantly.

There were some huge beetles that whistled by him, and one of them hit the elder bush with such force that its red berries all came off in a shower. The old rhinocerous beetle fell down, pretended to be dead, and did not dare to move. He realized that it was better to have nothing to do with those other beetles; there were too many of them whistling so loudly around him.

He lay there until the sun arose in the morning. Then the beetle opened one eye, and looked up at the sky. It was blue and warm, unlike anything he had ever seen in his village. Huge birds swooped screeching from the sky like kite-hawks. The beetle quickly turned round, stood up on his feet and crawled under a burdock, afraid that the kites might peck him to death.

That morning, Pyotr missed his beetle and started to look for him, probing the earth all around.

'What are you up to?' asked his friend, a soldier whose face was so sunburnt that you could have taken him for a black man.

'My beetle's gone away,' answered Pyotr. 'How terrible!'

'So that's all you're worried about,' said the bronzed soldier. 'It's only a beetle, you know. An insect. Insects have never been much use to a soldier.'

'It's not just a question of what's useful,' explained Pyotr. 'It's a memory. After all, it was my little boy who gave it to me. You see, my friend. It's not the insect that's so valuable. It's the memory.'

'Well, of course,' agreed the bronzed soldier. 'Obviously, that's another matter. But I doubt if you'll find it. It's like looking for a needle in a haystack. I reckon your beetle has gone missing.'

The old beetle heard Pyotr's voice, gave a buzz, lifted himself out of the earth, flew a few feet, and landed on the sleeve of Pyotr's greatcoat. Pyotr was overjoyed and laughed out loud. The bronzed soldier said, 'The old scoundrel! It comes to its master's voice like a dog.

Only an insect, but it knows what side its bread's buttered.'

From that day, Pyotr stopped keeping the beetle in the matchbox, and just carried him around in his gas-mask case. The other soldiers were even more surprised. 'Look,' they said, 'you've got that beetle tamed.'

When they had a bit of spare time, Pyotr would let his beetle out, and the beetle crawled around, digging out the odd little root or munching leaves. They were not quite the things he had been used to in his village. Instead of birch there were lots of elm and poplar leaves. And Pyotr would point out to his comrades: 'Look, he's making do with captured provisions.'

One evening, a breath of fresh air drifted into the gas mask, and the smell of a wide expanse of water. The beetle crawled out of the case to see where he had come to. Pyotr was standing with the other soldiers on the ferry, which was floating over the glistening river. The golden sun was setting over the banks covered with brittle-willows and cranes flew above them with their red feet.

'The Wisla!' shouted the soldiers, as they ladled the water with their canteens and drank. Some even washed their faces in the cool waves. 'We've already drunk the waters of the Don, the Dniepr and the Bug, and now we'll take a draught of the Wisla. The water of the Wisla is very sweet!'

The beetle breathed the air of the cold river, twirled his moustaches, crawled back into the bag and fell asleep.

He was awakened by a terrible shaking. The bag was jumping from side to side. The beetle crawled out quickly and looked around. Pyotr was running over a wheatfield and by his side the other soldiers ran cheering. The day had barely dawned, and the soldiers' helmets still sparkled with dew.

At first, the beetle clung on to the bag with all the

strength of its claws; then, realizing that he could not manage to hold on, he opened his wings, took off and flew alongside Pyotr, cheering him on, as it were, with his drone.

A man in a muddy-green uniform took aim at Pyotr with his gun, but the beetle swooped down and hit the man's eye. The man staggered, dropped his gun and ran for it.

The beetle flew behind Pyotr, landing on his shoulder and crawling into the bag only when Pyotr fell down on to the ground and cried out to someone: 'What bad luck! They've got me in the leg.' Just at that moment, people with muddy-green uniforms ran up, looking behind them, with the noisy hurrah of cheering at their heels.

Pyotr lay in the field-hospital for a month, and the beetle was given into the safe-keeping of a Polish boy. The boy lived in the yard where the field-hospital had been set up.

From the hospital, Pyotr went off to the Front again. His wound was not serious and he caught up with his unit in Germany. The smoke from the terrible battles was so thick that it seemed that the whole earth was on fire and every hollow threw up huge black clouds. Even the sun grew dim in the sky. The beetle was probably deafened by the thunder of the guns and sat in his bag without moving or making the slightest sound.

But one morning he stirred himself and crawled out. A warm breeze was blowing, taking with it far away to the south the last whisps of smoke. A bright sun shone high in the blue confines of the heavens. Everything was so still that the beetle heard the rustling of the leaves in the trees above him. All the leaves hung motionless. Only one fluttered and hummed, as if it was rejoicing in something and wanted to tell the other leaves about its joy.

Pyotr sat on the ground, drinking from a flask of

water. The drops streamed down his unshaven beard and reflected the sunlight. As he drank, Pyotr laughed and called out, 'Victory!'

'Victory!' echoed the soldiers who sat around.

One of them wiped his eyes with his sleeve and added, 'Glory for ever! Our motherland has yearned for our hands. We'll go and make a garden of it, and, brothers, we'll live free and happy.'

Soon after that, Pyotr returned home. Akulina squealed out and cried for joy, and Styopa cried as well and asked, 'Is the beetle still alive?'

'Yes, he's alive, my friend,' answered Pyotr. 'He wasn't even touched by a bullet. He's come back to his own place with the conquerors. And now we'll have to release him, Styopa.'

Pyotr took the beetle out of the bag and placed him on his palm.

The beetle sat still for a long while, looked around him, put out his whiskers, lifted himself up on to his hind legs, opened his wings, shut them again, thought a little, and then suddenly flew off with a great buzzing. He recognized his own land. He made a circle over the well, flew around the dill-bed in the vegetable patch, went over the river and the wood where the children called as they gathered mushrooms and wild raspberries. Styopa kept running after him, waving his cap.

'There you are,' said Pyotr, when Styopa returned. 'Now your old beetle will be telling his own folk about the war and his heroic adventures. He'll get all the beetles together under the juniper tree, and, bowing to his audience on all sides, he will tell his tale.'

Styopa laughed and Akulina said, 'Fancy telling a child such stories! He'll believe everything you say.'

'Well, let him believe it,' said Pyotr. 'It's not only children. Even soldiers can enjoy stories.'

'That may be so,' agreed Akulina, as she heaped pine-cones under the samovar.

The samovar bumbled like some old rhinocerous beetle. The blue smoke streamed from the funnel and drifted towards the evening sky, where the new moon stood, reflected in the lakes and rivers, looking from above on to our quiet and peaceful earth.

Chekhov

His notebooks live independently in literature as a special genre. He seldom used them for his work.

As an interesting genre, there exist the notebooks of Ilf, Alphonse Daudet, the diaries of Tolstoy, the Goncourt brothers, the French writer Renard, and a host of other notes penned by writers and poets.

Notebooks, as an independent genre, have a perfect right to exist in literature, but contrary to the opinion of many writers, I consider them almost useless for a major literary work.

For some time, I kept notebooks, but every time I took an interesting note from the book and inserted it into a novella or a short story, that piece of prose just looked devoid of life. It stuck out of the text like a sore thumb. I can explain this only from the fact that memory makes the best selection of material. What has remained in the memory and has not been forgotten is the most precious. Those things which are necessary to note, so that they will not be forgotten, are less valuable and are rarely of any use to the writer. Memory, like the magic sieve, lets the rubbish run through it, but preserves the grains of gold.

Chekhov had a second profession. He was a doctor. Obviously it would be useful for any writer to know another profession and to practise it from time to time.

Chekhov's being a doctor not only gave him a knowledge of people, but it even came through in his style. If Chekhov had not been a doctor, perhaps he would not have created such analytical and finely hewn prose, which was as incisive as a scalpel.

Some of his stories (for example, 'Ward No. 6', 'A Dreary Story', 'The Fidget', and indeed many others) are written like model pieces of psychological diagnosis.

His prose would not tolerate the slightest stain or speck of dust. 'One has to discard all that is superfluous,' wrote Chekhov, 'to rid the sentence of "to the extent of", "with the assistance of", and never to allow the juxtaposition of phrases like "she gave in" and "she gave up".'

He ruthlessly expunged from his prose French words like 'appetite', 'flirt', 'ideal', 'disc', 'écran'. These brought out loathing in him.

It is worth spreading out photographs of Chekhov over the years – from his early youth to the last period of his life – in order to see for oneself how, little by little, the light veneer of 'philistinism' vanished from his appearance, and how his face became more severe, considerably graver and finer, and how his dress became progressively more elegant and informal.

In this country of ours, there is a corner where all of us keep a piece of our heart. That is the Chekhov house at Autka in Yalta. For people of my generation that house is like a window lit from inside. Standing before it, it is possible to see from the dark garden one's half-forgotten childhood, and to hear the voice of Maria Pavlovna,[13] Chekhov's dearest Masha[14], whom almost the whole country knows and loves like a blood-relation.

The last time I was in that house was 1949.

Maria Pavlovna and I were sitting on the low terrace.

Brakes of white scented flowers hid the sea and Yalta. Maria Pavlovna said that Anton Pavlovich had planted that magnificently spreading bush. He had called it something, but she could not remember the strange name he had given it.

She said it so simply, as if Chekhov was still alive, as if he had been there a little while ago, and had gone away for some time to Moscow, Nice or somewhere.

I picked a camellia from Chekhov's garden and presented it to a little girl who was with us at Maria Pavlovna's house. But that careless *Dame aux Camélias* dropped the flower from the bridge into the mountain river Uchan-Su, and it floated off to the Black Sea. I could not be angry with her, especially on that day when, so it seemed, at every turn of the street we might meet Chekhov. And he would not have been pleased to hear how we scolded a confused little girl with grey eyes for such a trifle as a flower lost from his garden.

1955

Aleksandr Blok *

In Blok there are some early, little known poems: collected as *The Warm Night Clothed the Islands*.

Among these poems there is one protracted and gentle line, which evokes in the memory all the wonder of misty youth:

Spring of my distant dreams . . .

These are not just words; they are a revelation. From such revelations the whole of Blok is made up.

Every time I used to go to Leningrad, I wanted to go to the Pryazhka (to go on foot, I mean, not by the bus or the tram) to find the house where Blok lived and died.

One day, I was walking and lost myself among the deserted blocks of flats and the canals covered with slime; even so I never found Blok's house. But just by chance, in a narrow street, overgrown with grass, I saw a memorial plaque on a faded brick building. It appeared that Dostoyevsky had lived in that house.

Just recently I found Blok's house at last on the embankment of the River Pryazhka.

* Aleksandr Blok (1880–1921), one of Russia's most famous lyric poets

The late autumn had scattered heaps of dry leaves over the black river. On the other side of the Pryazhka began the working-class dock area of the city. From there could be seen factories, shipyards, the masts of steamers, smoke, the pale late-afternoon sky. But on the Pryazhka it was deserted and silent, as in some far-flung province.

This was a strange refuge for a poet like Blok. Perhaps Blok searched for this silence near the sea because it gives back calm to the turbulent human heart.

1955

The Life of Aleksandr
Grin *

In 1924, Grin moved to Feodosiya. He wished to live quietly near his beloved sea. By doing this he reflected the writer's true instinct – life by the sea was for him that really fertile soil which gave him the opportunity of inventing his stories.

Grin lived in Feodosiya until 1930. He wrote a great deal there, mainly during the winter in the mornings. Sometimes he would sit in his armchair for hours on end, smoking and thinking, and at that time no one could disturb him. During those hours of deep thought, when he was giving free play to his imagination, complete concentration was much more important to Grin than it was during his working hours. Grin sank so deeply into his meditation that he was almost deaf and blind, and to bring him out of this state was difficult.

In the summer, Grin would rest. He would make bows, wander by the sea, look after stray dogs, tame a wounded hawk, read and play billiards with the light-hearted inhabitants of Feodosiya, descendants of Geno-

* Aleksandr Grin (1880–1932), a famous Soviet romantic novelist

ese and Greeks. He loved Feodosiya – a sultry town by the green, turbid sea, built on white stony earth.

In the autumn of 1930, Grin moved from Feodosiya to Stary Krim, a town of flowers, calm and ruins. Here he died in solitude of an agonising disease – cancer of the stomach and lungs.

Grin died as hard as he had lived. He asked for his bed to be placed by the window, from which in the distance could be seen the blue mountains of the Crimea and the sky sparkling like the gleam of his beloved sea now lost for ever.

In one of Grin's stories, 'The Return', there are a few lines which might have been written of his own death, so accurately do they describe the circumstances in which he died: *The end came in the light from the open windows before the face of the meadow-flowers. Already gasping for breath, he asked to be placed by the window. He looked towards the hills, catching the last gulps of air with the remaining scrap of his bleeding lung.*

Before his death, Grin began to miss people extremely – something that had never happened to him earlier.

A few days before he died, he was sent from Leningrad the author's copies of his last book *An Autobiographical Story*. He smiled feebly, tried to read the inscription on the dust-jacket, but could not. The book fell from his hands. His eyes had already taken on that deep, opaque expression of vacancy. Grin's eyes, which had had the power to see the world in such an unusual fashion, were already dead.

His last words, uttered either with a groan or with a whisper, were, 'I'm dying . . .'

Two years after Grin's death, I happened to be in Stary Krim, in the house where he died, and by his grave.

Around the small, white house among the thick, fresh

grass, bloomed meadow-flowers. The leaves of the walnut tree, withered by the heat, smelt like acrid medicine. In the rooms furnished with simple severity stood a deep silence, and a sharp sunbeam played on the chalk wall. It fell upon the only print attached to it – a portrait of Edgar Allan Poe.

In the cemetery, behind an old mosque, his grave was overgrown with spiky grass.

The wind was blowing from the south. Very far away, on the other side of Feodosiya, stood the sea like a blue-grey wall. And over everything – over Grin's house, over his grave, over Stary Krim – stood the hush of a cloudless summer's day.

Grin died leaving us to resolve the question: Does our age really need such tempestuous dreamers as he was?

Yes, we do need dreamers. It is time to be rid of the sarcastic connotation of this word. Many people are still not able to dream, and that may be because they cannot stand on a level with this age.

If the ability to dream is taken away from a person, then he is robbed of one of the most powerful, one of the most stimulating causes which gives birth to culture, art and science, and the desire to do battle in the name of a glorious future is taken away from him. But dreams must not be divorced from reality; they must foresee the future and create in us the feeling that we already live in that future and that we are ourselves already becoming different.

It is usually thought that Grin's dreams were apart from life, that they appear whimsical, a senseless sport of the mind. It is often held that Grin was a writer of adventure, certainly a master of plot, but a man whose books were devoid of social meaning.

The significance of any writer is defined by the way he attracts us, by the feelings, thoughts and actions which his books evoke; have they enriched us with knowledge or are they read merely like an amusing collection of words?

Grin populated his books with hordes of bold people, innocent as children – proud, selfless, good people.

These worthy, attractive people are surrounded by the pure, fragrant air of Grin's nature – completely real, touching the heart with its charm. The world in which Grin's heroes live can seem unreal only to the person of mean spirit. Anyone who has experienced the light spinning of the head from the very first gulp of the salty, warm air of the seashore will at once feel the authenticity of Grin's landscape, the wide breadth of Grin's countries.

Grin's stories evoke in people the desire for a varied life, full of risk, boldness and a 'feeling for the supreme', characteristic of researchers, seafarers and travellers. After his stories, one wishes to see the whole globe – not the countries thought up by Grin, but those that are real, actual, full of light, woods, the multilingual babble of harbours, human passion and love.

'The earth lures me,' wrote Grin. 'Its vast oceans, uncountable islands and the array of mysterious, deadly curious corners.'

A tale is necessary not only for children, but also for grown-ups. It brings out agitation – the source of mighty, human passions. It does not allow us to relax, but always shows new, sparkling horizons, another life; it is demanding and makes us long passionately for such a life. In this is its value, and in this is the value of the fascination of Grin's stories, a fascination as yet unable to be expressed in words, but clear and powerful.

Our age has declared merciless war on sanctimonious hypocrites, blockheads and dissemblers. Only a hypocrite can say that we should acquiesce in what has been achieved and then stop. Glorious is our achievement, but in the future awaits one even more glorious. New tasks, lofty and serious, stand on the nearest horizon of the future – the problems of the creation of a new man, the fostering of new feelings and new human relationships worthy of the socialist age. But in order to struggle for this future, we must be capable of dreaming passionately, deeply and effectively; we must nurture in ourselves a constant desire for the intelligent and the wonderful. Grin was rich in this desire, and he passes it on to us in his books.

People talk of adventure being the only subject of Grin. It is true, but with him the subject of adventure is only a shell for a much deeper content. You would have to be blind not to see in Grin's work love for mankind.

Grin was not only a splendid landscape painter and a master of the subject; he was a very shrewd psychologist. He wrote about self-sacrifice, fortitude – heroic traits to be found in the most ordinary people. He wrote of love for labour, for one's own profession, of the 'unlearnability' and power of nature. Finally very few writers wrote so purely, carefully and anxiously of love for a woman as did Grin.

Here I could adduce hundreds of extracts from Grin's books, which would excite anyone who has not lost the ability to become perturbed before the sight of the exquisite, but the reader will find them for himself.

Grin used to say that 'the whole earth with everything it contains is given to us for living our life, for the recognition of this life wherever it is to be found'.

Grin is a writer necessary for our age, for he made his contribution to the cause of the nurturing of lofty feelings, without which the realization of a socialist society is impossible.

1939–56

Maxim Gorky

So much has been written about Alexei Maximovich Gorky that, were it not for his greatness, it would be easy to be embarrassed, to step back and not add one line to all that has been said about him.

Gorky occupies a great place in the life of all of us. I am even inclined to say there exists a 'feeling of Gorky', a sense of his continuing presence in our lives. In Gorky, for me, resides the whole of Russia. I can no more imagine Russia without the Volga than I can think that there is no Gorky in it.

He was the most powerful representative of the boundlessly talented Russian people. He loved his country and knew it from top to bottom; he knew it, as geologists might say, from every angle both in space and time; there was nothing in it that he would have neglected, nor that he did not see in his very own way – through the eyes of Gorky.

He was a seeker of talent, a man with his finger on the pulse of his age. From people like Gorky we might even begin a new era.

The first time I met him I was immediately struck by his unusually elegant outward appearance, in spite of his slight stoop and hardly audible speech. He had reached that stage of spiritual growth and maturity when inner perfection imposes an indelible stamp on the exterior – on gestures, on the mode of speaking and dressing, in short on the whole appearance of a man.

This elegance, united with a force of self-confidence, was noticeable in his widely spread hands, in his attentive glance, in the way he walked and in the suit which he wore nonchalantly, or even with artistic carelessness. In my mind's eye, I often see him as he was described to me by a writer who had been staying with Gorky at Tesseli in the Crimea.

The writer woke up very early one morning and went over to the window. In the distance, a gale was blowing over the sea. There was an unabating, resilient south wind howling through the gardens and whistling by the weather-cocks. Not far from the small house where the writer was staying grew a huge poplar tree. Gogol might have called it 'a poplar reaching up to heaven'. And there by the poplar, the writer saw Gorky leaning on his cane, his head tilted upwards, gazing intently at the powerful tree. The heavy dense foliage of the poplar shook and rustled in the gale. The leaves continually tossed by the wind were turned up to reveal their silvery underside. The tree vibrated like a gigantic organ. Gorky removed his hat and for a long time stood motionless looking at the poplar. At last he said something and walked off into the depths of the garden, occasionally stopping to look back.

At dinner, the writer found the courage to ask Gorky what he had said by the poplar. Without a hint of surprise, Gorky answered, 'Well, since you were spying on me, I might as well confess. I said. "What power!" '

Once I was staying with Alexei Maximovich at his house in Gorki outside Moscow. It was a summer's day, and the curly, light clouds were tinged with colour, throwing their shadow on to the green hills beyond the river; a warm breeze blew through the rooms.

Gorky was talking to me about my latest novel, *Kolkhida*, imagining me to be an expert on the nature of the subtropics. This greatly embarrassed me. Even so, we got into an argument about whether dogs suffered from malaria. Finally, Gorky yielded and with a kindly smile mentioned an episode from his life when he was in Poti – a town in Georgia – and saw chickens suffering from malaria with their feathers rumpled, painfully squawking.

He spoke, employing language so clear and rich that none of us these days could aspire to such words.

I had just finished reading an extremely rare book, written by one of our seafarers, Captain Gernet, entitled *Lichens of the Ice*. At one time, Gernet had been the Soviet naval representative in Japan and had written his book there. Unable to find a Japanese compositor who knew Russian he had set the type himself and had brought out in all five-hundred copies on fine Japanese paper.

In the book, Captain Gernet had proposed an ingenious theory concerning the re-establishment of the subtropical Miocene climate in Europe. In the Miocene Age, it appeared, magnolia and cypress forests had flourished on the Gulf of Finland, and even at Spitzbergen.

Here I cannot give a detailed account of Gernet's theories, since this would take up far too much space, but suffice it to say that he had proved conclusively that if it were possible to melt the Greenland ice-cap, Europe would revert to the Miocene Age and nature would be once more on the threshold of a new, golden era.

The only weakness of the theory was the obvious impossibility of melting the Greenland ice-cap. In this modern age, with the discovery of atomic power, we may, if you wish, entertain such ideas!

I told Gorky of Gernet's theory. He was drumming with his fingers on the table, and it seemed to me he was listening only out of politeness. But it turned out that he was fascinated by the harmonious irrefutability of the theory and even by the kind of solemnity it contained.

He discussed it for a long time, becoming more and more animated, and asked me to send him a copy of the book in order that he might bring out an extensive edition of it in Russia. He spoke at length about the number of intellectual and pleasant surprises which lie in wait for us at every step we make.

But Alexei Maximovich never succeeded in having Gernet's book published. He died soon afterwards.

1955

The Old Cook

It was a winter evening in the year 1786. In a small wooden house on the outskirts of Vienna an old blind man was dying. At one time he had been a cook in the service of the Countess Thun. It was really not much of a house – just a tumbledown old watchman's hut, standing in the depths of the garden. The garden was strewn with rotting twigs, thrown down by the wind. The twigs crunched under every footstep, and then in his kennel the watchdog would growl softly. Like his master, he was also dying from old age and could no longer bark.

Some years previously, the cook had been blinded by the heat of the stove. After that, the Countess's estate-manager had given him a place in the watchman's hut and occasionally handed him a few florins.

Together with the cook lived his daughter, Maria, a young girl of about eighteen. The entire furniture of the watchman's hut consisted of a bed, some lame benches, a rough table, a few glazed earthenware utensils covered with cracks, and finally a harpsichord – Maria's only wealth.

The harpsichord was so old that its strings would reverberate long and quietly in answer to any sound made around it. The cook jokingly called the harpsichord 'the watchman of the house'. No one could enter without the instrument greeting the newcomer with a quivering and senile hum.

As Maria washed her father and dressed him in a cold, clean nightshirt, the old man said, 'I've never had much time for priests and monks; I can't call a confessor; but even so before I die I must unburden my conscience.'

'What can we do?' asked Maria, alarmed.

'Go out into the street,' said the old man, 'and ask the first person you meet to come into our house and hear the confession of a dying man. No one will refuse you.'

'Our street is so deserted...' murmured Maria, as she threw on her shawl and went out.

She ran across the garden, with difficulty opened the rusty gate and stopped. The street was empty. The wind blew the leaves around her, and from the dark sky drops of rain began to fall.

Maria waited for a long time and listened intently. Finally it seemed to her that a person was walking along by the fence, humming. She took a few steps towards him, collided with him and cried out. The man stopped and asked: 'Who's there?'

Maria grabbed his hand and in a quavering voice delivered her father's request.

'Very well,' said the man quietly. 'Although I am not a priest, it does not matter. Let us go!'

They entered the house. In the candlelight Maria saw a small, thin man. He threw his wet cape down on to a bench. He was elegantly but simply dressed. The flame of the candle picked out the crystal buttons on his black waistcoat and lace shirt-front.

He was still very young – this stranger. Just like an adolescent, he tossed back his head, adjusted his powdered wig, quickly drew a stool up to the bed, sat down and, bending forward, gazed with intensity and kindness into the face of the dying man.

'Tell me,' he said. 'Perhaps with the power given to me not by God but by the art which I serve, I can make your last moments easier and take away the burden from your soul.'

'All my life I worked until I was blinded,' whispered the old man, taking the stranger by the hand and drawing him nearer to himself. 'And one who works has no time to sin. When my wife – her name was Marta – was taken ill with consumption, and the physician prescribed various expensive medicines for her and ordered me to feed her with cream and dried figs, and to give her hot red wine to drink, I stole a gold dish from the Countess Thun's service, broke it into pieces and sold it. And now it is hard for me to face what I did, and to hide it from my daughter. I brought her up never to touch a crumb from another's table.'

'And did any of the countess's servants suffer by it?' asked the stranger.

'I swear to you, sir, no one,' answered the old man, the tears coming into his eyes. 'If I had known that gold would not help my Marta, do you think I could ever have stolen?'

'What is your name? asked the stranger.

'Johann Meyer, sir.'

'Very well, Johann Meyer,' said the stranger, placing the palm of his hand over the blind eyes of the old man. 'You are innocent in the sight of the world. What you did is neither a sin nor is it counted as a theft. On the contrary, it can be counted as a deed of love.'

'Amen,' whispered the old man.

'Amen,' echoed the stranger. 'And now tell me what is your last wish?'

'I want somebody to take care of Maria.'

'I shall see to that. What else do you wish?'

The dying man smiled unexpectedly and cried out, 'I should like to see Marta once more just as I met her when we were young. I should like to see the sun and

148

the old garden bursting into flower in the springtime. But that is not possible, sir. Do not be impatient with me for my stupid words. It must be my illness that has driven me out of my senses.'

'Very well,' said the stranger, standing up. 'Very well,' he repeated, walked over to the harpsichord and sat down on the stool before it. 'Very well,' he said loudly for the third time, and suddenly a rapid melody spread over the hut, as if a myriad crystal fragments had been strewn over the floor.

'Listen,' said the stranger. 'Listen and watch!'

He played on. Afterwards, Maria recalled the stranger's face when the first note reverberated under his hands. An extraordinary pallor covered his forehead and the flame of the candle played in his darkening eyes.

The harpsichord sang at the top of its voice, the first time for many years. With its sounds it filled not only the hut but the whole garden. The old dog climbed out of its kennel, sat up inclining its head to one side, and pricking up its ears gently began to wag its tail. Wet snow began to fall but the dog only twitched its ears.

'I can see, sir!' exclaimed the old man and propped himself up in bed. I can see the day when I met Marta, and she was so embarrassed that she broke a jug of milk. It was winter in the mountains. The sky was transparent like blue glass, and Marta was laughing. She was laughing,' he repeated, listening intently to the murmur of the strings.

The stranger played on, gazing through the black window. 'And now,' he asked, 'do you see anything?'

The old man was silent as he listened.

'Surely you can see,' said the stranger excitedly, not stopping his playing, 'that the black of the night has turned to dark blue, and now it turns to azure. The warm light is already descending from above and the old branches of your trees are blossoming into white flowers. I think it must be apple-blossom, though from here in the room they resemble large tulips. You see how the first sunbeam has fallen on the stone wall, warming it, and steam is rising from it. The moss covered with melting snow must be drying. The sky becomes still higher, bluer and more serene, and flocks of birds are already flying northwards to our old Vienna.'

'I can see it all,' cried the old man.

The pedal gently creaked, and the harpsichord sang out triumphantly, not as one instrument, but like hundreds of exultant voices.

'No, sir,' said Maria to the stranger. 'Those flowers are not at all like tulips. They are apple trees bursting into bloom in only one night.'

'Yes,' answered the stranger, 'they are apple trees, but the petals of the flowers are very large.'

'Open the window, Maria,' asked the old man.

Maria opened the window and the cold air burst into the room. The stranger was playing very softly and slowly.

The old man fell back on to the pillows, breathed greedily and groped with his hands over the blankets. Maria rushed towards him. The stranger stopped playing. He sat without a movement at the harpsichord, as if bewitched by his own music.

Maria cried out. The stranger stood up and walked over to the bed. Gasping for breath the old man said, 'I saw everything, as clearly as I saw it many years ago. But I should not wish to die without knowing . . . your name. Your name!'

'My name is Wolfgang Amadeus Mozart,' answered the stranger.

Maria moved away from the bed, and almost touching the floor with her knee, she bowed low before the great musician. When she straightened herself up, the old man was already dead. The dawn flared up in the windows, and in its light stood the garden, strewn with the blossoms of wet snow.

1940

The Creaking Floorboards

Beauty of midnight nature,
Love of the eyes,
My country!

                              Yazykov[15]

The house was cracked by old age. It could also have
been because it stood in a pine-wood clearing and,
throughout the whole summer, heat wafted from the
pines. Sometimes the wind blew but it did not even
penetrate the open windows in the attic. It just moaned
in the tops of the pines, and carried above them lines
of fluffy clouds.

Tchaikovsky loved this wooden house. The rooms
smelt faintly of turpentine and white carnations. They
blossomed in abundance in the clearing before the
porch. Tousled, dried up, they did not even look like
flowers, but rather reminded one of tufts of down, stuck
to the stems.

The only thing that annoyed the composer was the
creaking floorboards. To get from the door to the piano
he had to step across five of these unsteady boards.
From the side, it must have looked funny as the elderly
composer picked his way to the piano, examining the
boards with screwed-up eyes.

Thank God, not one of them creaked! Tchaikovsky
sat at the piano and smiled. The unpleasant was left
behind, and now the surprising and the pleasant was
about to start. The cracked house would sing out from
the very first sounds of the piano; its dry rafters, the
doors and the old chandelier missing half its crystal

fittings, which resembled oak leaves, would call out to any note with the finest resonance.

The simplest musical theme would be performed by the house like a symphony. 'A wonderful orchestration!' thought Tchaikovsky, carried away by the song of the wood.

For some time, Tchaikovsky had begun to feel that from early morning the house was waiting for him to drink his coffee and take his place at the piano. It missed the sounds.

Sometimes at night, when waking up, he would listen to the floorboards, now one, then another, creaking as if they were recalling his music of the daytime, and plucking from it their favourite note. This also reminded him of the orchestra before the overture, when the players tune their instruments. One here, one there, one in the loft, one in the mirrored lobby, one in the small hall – someone was touching a string. Through his sleep, Tchaikovsky caught a melody, but when he awoke in the morning, he had already forgotten it. He would strain his memory and sigh. What a shame now not to be able to play the nocturnal strumming of the wooden house, the uncomplicated song of the dry wood, of the window-panes with their flaking putty, the wind, knocking with a branch on the roof.

Listening to the sounds of the night, he would fancy that life passes by like that, and nothing much is accomplished. All that had been written was just an exercise, a meagre offering to his people, to his friends and to his favourite poet, Aleksandr Sergeevich Pushkin. But he had never succeeded in imparting that light rapture, which springs from the pageant of the rainbow, from the calling of the village girls in the thickets, from the simple occurrences of the life around us.

The simpler the things he saw, the harder it was to capture them in music. How, for instance, might he have expressed something that happened yesterday, when he took shelter from the pouring rain in the cabin of the forester, Tikhon? Tikhon's daughter, Fenya, a girl of about fifteen, ran into the cabin with rain dripping from her hair, and two drops hung from the lobes of her small ears. The sun broke through the cloud, and the raindrops gleamed on Fenya's ears like diamond earrings.

Tchaikovsky looked fondly at the girl, but when Fenya shook off the drops, all was over, and he realized the impossibility of expressing the delight of those fleeting drops in any sort of music.

And Fet* said in his verse: 'Only for you, poet, can the winged sound of a word catch in flight and suddenly fix the sombre ravings of the soul and the vague scent of the grass . . .'

No, this was apparently not granted to him. He had never waited for inspiration. He went on working like a day-labourer, like a bullock, and inspiration was born from the work.

What really helped him most of all were the woods, this house set among them, where he was staying, the cuttings in the forest, the thickets, the neglected roads, where, in their ruts filled with rain, the crescent moon was reflected in the twilight – this amazing air and the Russian sunsets, always a bit sad.

He would not exchange these misty dawns for all the gilded sunsets of Paris. He had given his heart without reserve to Russia, to its woods and its little villages, to their outskirts, to its paths and its songs. But with every passing day, the impossibility of expressing all the poetry of his country disturbed him. He must overcome it. Only he must have no mercy upon himself.

Fortunately, in life wonderful days occur – just like today. He woke up very early and for a few moments lay still, listening to the woodlarks calling to one

* Afanasy Fet (1820–98), a famous Russian lyric poet

another. Even without looking through the window, he knew that dew-filled shadows lay in the wood. On the neighbouring pine, a cuckoo called. He got up, walked over to the window and began to smoke. The house stood on a hillock. The woods went down into the happy distance, where among the thickets was a lake. This was his favourite place – it was called Rudy Yar, the 'Red Ravine'.

The very road to the ravine always called up excitement. Once in winter at the damp hotel in Rome, he had woken up during the night and had started to recall the way step by step: first through the cutting where near the stumps the pink rose-day blossomed; then the birch forest, rich in mushrooms; then onwards across the broken bridge over the stream in the glades; then upwards along the gentle slope to the coniferous forest which yields timber for ships. He recalled that journey and his heart beat painfully. This place seemed to him by far the best expression of Russian nature.

He called the servant and hurried him, so that he could wash quickly, drink his coffee and go to Rudy Yar. He knew that by being there today, he would return – and that favourite theme, so long suppressed somewhere inside him, the theme of the lyric strength of that part of the forest, would spill over and come gushing out in endless streams of sound. In a year's time, he would be amazed by what he had written.

And so it happened. For a long time he stood on the precipice of Rudy Yar. Dew dripped from lime and birch brakes. All around, the damp gleam was so strong that it made him screw up his eyes.

But more than anything on that day, it was the light that struck Tchaikovsky. He gazed at it and now saw new layers of light falling on the familiar woods. Why had he not noticed it before? The light streamed from the sky in straight torrents, and under the light, seen from above, from the ravine, the tops of the forest seemed especially prominent and curly.

Upon the edge of the wood the beams of light fell obliquely and the nearest pine-trunks were of the same gentle golden shade as delicate pine-boards, illuminated from behind by a candle. And on that morning, with unusually clear sight, he noticed that the pine-trunks also cast their light on the undergrowth and on the grass – so faint, but of the same golden, pinkish tone. And lastly, he saw today how the willow- and alder-thickets over the lake were lit from below by the bluish gleam of the water.

The familiar land was all bathed in light, even to the last blade of grass. The variety and the power of the illumination evoked in Tchaikovsky that feeling when it seems that something unusual is going to happen, something resembling a miracle. He had experienced that feeling before. He must not lose it. He must go home at once, sit at his piano, and without delay write down what he had played on sheets of lined paper.

Tchaikovsky quickly reached the house. In the clearing stood the tall, spreading pine, which he called his 'lighthouse'. Without stopping he ran his hand over its warmed bark. It rustled quietly, even though it was not windy.

Once home, he ordered his servant to let no one in, went into the small hall, locked the creaking door and sat down at the piano.

1948

The Basket of Fir-Cones

The composer Edward Grieg was spending the autumn in the woods near Bergen.

All woods are good with their mushroomy air and their rustling leaves, but especially good are the mountainous woods near the sea. In them you can hear the noise of the breakers. Mist constantly arises from the sea and moss grows quickly from the abundance of the moisture, tumbling in green swathes from the branches to the very ground. As well as that, in these woods, like a mocking-bird, lives a gay echo, existing only to catch any sound and hurl it back through the rocks.

One day in the woods, Grieg met a little girl with two plaits, the daughter of a woodsman. In her basket she was collecting fir-cones.

It was autumn. And if it were possible to collect all the gold and copper that exists in the world, and to mould from it thousands and thousands of slender leaves, they would form only a tiny part of that autumnal raiment which clothed the hills. Moreover, these beaten leaves would appear coarse in comparison with the real ones, especially with the leaves of the aspen. As everyone knows, aspen leaves tremble even at the whistle of a bird.

'What's your name, little girl?' asked Grieg.

'Dagni Pedersen,' answered the girl in a loud voice.

She answered loudly, not from fear but from confusion. She could not have been afraid because Grieg's eyes were laughing.

'What a pity I've got nothing to give you as a present,' said Grieg. 'In my pocket I have no dolls, no ribbons, no velvet hares.'

'I've got an old doll that belonged to my mummy,' answered the girl. 'Once she used to close her eyes. Like this!'

The girl slowly closed her eyes. When she opened them again, Grieg noticed that her pupils were greenish and the leaves were reflected in them like little lights.

'But now she sleeps with her eyes open,' added Dagni sadly. 'Old people sleep badly. Granpapa wheezes all night as well.'

'Listen, Dagni,' said Grieg. 'I've had a thought. I'll give you something interesting. Only not now. I'll give it to you in about ten years' time.'

Dagni clasped her hands. 'Oh! So long!'

'You see. I've still got to make it.'

'And what's that?'

'You'll find out later.'

'You mean in the whole of your life you'll be able to make only five or six toys?' asked Dagni reproachfully.

Grieg was embarrassed.

'No, no! Not quite!' he objected without conviction. 'I might manage it in a few days. But the things I have in mind aren't given to little children. I make presents for grown-ups.'

'I shan't break it,' said Dagni, pleading and tugging at Grieg's sleeve. 'And I shan't destroy it. You'll see. Grandpapa's got a toy boat made of glass. I dust it and I've never once snapped the tiniest part from it.'

'She's really cornered me, this Dagni,' thought Grieg with some dismay, and he addressed her as grown-ups always address children when they find themselves beaten and in an awkward position: 'You're still small and there are lots of things you don't understand. You'll have to learn to wait. Now give me your basket. You can hardly carry it. I'll take you home and we'll talk about something else'.

Dagni sighed and handed the basket to Grieg. It was really heavy. Fir-cones contain a lot of resin and so weigh far more than pine-cones.

When the woodman's house finally came into sight among the trees, Grieg said, 'Here we are. Now you run along by yourself, Dagni Pedersen. In Norway a lot of little girls have the same name as you. What's your father's name?'

'Hagerup,' answered Dagni, and knitting her brows said: 'Aren't you coming in? We've got an embroidered tablecloth, a tabby cat and a glass boat. Granpapa will let you pick it up.'

'Thank you, but I have no time at the moment. Goodbye, Dagni.'

Grieg smoothed the little girl's hair and walked in the direction of the sea. Dagni, frowning, watched him go. She tucked the basket under her arm and the fir-cones tumbled out of it.

'I'll write her some music', Grieg decided. 'On the title-page I'll put the dedication: *To Dagni Pedersen, daughter of the woodcutter, Hagerup Pedersen, for her eighteenth birthday.*

In Bergen all was as he had left it. Grieg had long since removed everything from the house that might stifle sound – rugs, curtains and soft-furnishings. Only an old sofa remained. It could seat up to ten guests and Grieg did not dare to throw it away.

Friends used to say that the composer's house resembled the dwelling of a woodcutter. It was embellished only by a grand piano. Anyone endowed with imagination might have heard magical things between those white walls – anything from the rumbling of the northern ocean, rolling its waves along from the gloom of the wind which whistled its wild saga over them, to the song of a small girl singing lullabies to her rag-doll.

The piano could sing about anything, about the surges of the human soul towards greatness and love. The white and black keys, dashing under Grieg's strong fingers, were melancholy, then laughed, thundered with the rage of a storm and suddenly fell silent.

Then in the hush, only one small string prolonged its sound, as if a Cinderella, hurt by her sisters, were still weeping.

Moving away, Grieg would listen until the last sound fell silent in the kitchen, where a cricket had long since taken up residence.

The only thing that could then be heard was the dripping tap counting the seconds with the precision of a metronome. The drips were a reminder that time does not wait and that one must hurry to accomplish all that had been thought of.

Grieg spent more than a month writing Dagni Pedersen's music.

Winter began. The mist wrapped the city up to the throat. Rusty steamers arrived from different countries, dozed by the wooden jetties, peacefully wheezed out their smoke.

Soon it began to snow. Grieg watched it from his window flying obliquely, clinging to the tops of the trees.

However rich our language might be, it would be impossible to express the music in words. Grieg was writing about the deepest charms and the happiness of maidenhood. He was writing and seeing a young girl, with radiant green eyes, running towards him out of breath with joy. She clings to his neck, putting her warm cheek against his grey, unshaven face. 'Thank you', she says, not knowing herself why she is so grateful to him.

'You are like the sun,' Grieg says to her. 'Like the soft wind and the early morning. A white flower has blossomed in your heart and has filled your whole being with the fragrance of the spring. I have seen life. Whatever they tell you about it, always believe that it is full of surprises and wonder. I am an old man, but I have given to youth life, work and talent. I gave everything, hoping for no return. Therefore, I am perhaps even happier than you, Dagni.

'You are a white night with its mysterious light. You are happiness. You are the gleam of the dawn. The heart starts up at the sound of your voice.

'Let everything that surrounds you be blessed – everything that touches you and everything that is touched by you; all that gladdens you and all that makes you think.'

Such were Grieg's thoughts as he played everything that went through his mind. He suspected that he was being overheard by someone. He even guessed who it might be – the tits in the trees, sailors on a spree from the port, the laundress from the neighbouring house, the cricket, the snow flying down from the overcast sky, and Cinderella in her patched dress.

All listened in their own way.

The tits were anxious. No matter how much they gyrated, their chatter could not muffle the piano. The boozy sailors sprawled around the steps of the house and listened, sobbing. The laundress straightened her back, wiped her reddened eyes with her palms and shook her head. The cricket crawled out from his crack in the tiled stove, and observed Grieg through the chink.

The falling snow halted and hung in the air to listen to the sound streaming from the house. And Cinderella smiled and looked down at the floor. By her bare feet stood the crystal slippers. They shuddered and knocked against each other in answer to the chords flying from Grieg's room.

Grieg prized this audience much more highly than the smart, polite visitors to his concerts.

Dagni finished school at the age of eighteen.

On that occasion her father sent her along to Christiania[16] to visit his sister, Magda. My little girl – the father still thought of her as a little girl, even though Dagni was already a shapely young lady with heavy light-brown plaits – let her see what the world looks like and how the people live, and cheer herself up!

Who knows what awaits Dagni in the future? Perhaps an honest and loving but parsimonious and boring husband? Or working as an assistant in a village shop? Or service in one of those numerous steamer offices in Bergen?

Magda worked as a dressmaker for the theatre. Her husband, Nils, served the same establishment as a hairdresser. They lived in a little room under the theatre roof, from which one could see the bay decorated with coloured seafaring flags and the statue of Ibsen.

All day long, the steamers bellowed out into the open windows, and Nils had learnt their voices so well that, as he said, he could tell them apart without making a mistake – the *Nordic Belle* from Copenhagen, the *Scottish Bard* from Glasgow or the *Jeanne d'Arc* from Bordeaux.

In Aunt Magda's room there were plenty of theatrical effects: brocades, silks, tuiles, ribbons, laces, old felt hats with black ostrich feathers, gypsy shawls, grey wigs, jackboots with bronze spurs, swords, fans and silver slippers worn at the creases. All these things had arrived to be stitched, mended, cleaned and ironed.

On the walls there were pictures cut out of books

and magazines: cavaliers of the time of Ludovic XIV, beauties in crinolines, knights, Russian women in sarafans, sailors and Vikings with oak wreathes on their heads.

To reach the room, you had to go up a steep staircase, and there was always the smell of paint and gilt lacquer.

Dagni often went to the theatre. This was a fascinating experience. But after the show she often could not get to sleep, and sometimes even cried in bed. Worried by this, Aunt Magda would calm her down and tell her that she must not believe unquestioningly everything that had been enacted upon the stage. But Uncle Nils got at Magda for being like a 'broody hen', and stated that, on the contrary, in the theatre you should believe everything. Otherwise no one would need the theatre. Dagni went on believing, but even so Aunt Magda insisted that for a change they should go to concerts instead.

Nils did not fight against this. 'Music,' he said, 'is the mirror of genius.'

Nils liked to express himself in such an elevated and vague fashion. He would say about Dagni that she was like the first chord of an overture. And Magda, to quote his words, had a bewitching power over people. This came from the fact that she stitched theatrical costumes, and all knew that every time a man was put into a new guise he changed completely. And so it happened that one and the same actor yesterday was a vile murderer, today he had become an ardent lover, tomorrow he would be a king's jester, and the day after a people's hero.

'Dagni!' Aunt Magda would cry out on such occasions, 'stop your ears and don't listen to his awful drivel. He doesn't know what he's talking about, that homespun philosopher!'

It was a warm evening. The white nights had come.

The concerts were in full swing in the city park under the open sky.

Dagni went to the concert with her aunt and uncle, and wanted to wear her only white dress. But Nils said that a pretty girl should dress in such a way as to distinguish herself from the surrounding decor. His long tirade on this subject amounted to no more than that on white nights you should dress in black and on dark ones the dress should dazzle with its whiteness.

It was impossible to argue with Nils, and Dagni put on a black dress of silky-soft velvet. She had acquired it from the costume wardrobe. When Dagni put on the dress, Magda agreed that Nils was right after all; nothing set off the severe lines of Dagni's pale face and her long hair which glinted like burnished gold so well as that mysterious velvet.

'Look, Magda!' said Nils softly. 'Dagni is as beautiful as if she were going out to her first assignation!'

'Yes, quite so!' answered Magda. 'It's only that *I* didn't see such a dashing figure before me when you came to meet me for the first time. All you were was a chatterbox!' Magda kissed Uncle Nils on the head.

The concert began after the usual evening firing of the old canon in the port, which marked the setting of the sun. Regardless of the evening, neither the conductor nor the orchestra put on the lamps over their stands. The evening was so bright that the arc-lamps burning in the lime trees were apparently there just to give the concert some decorum.

For the first time, Dagni heard symphonic music, which produced a strange effect upon her. The modulations and beats of the orchestra conjured up for Dagni a host of pictures like dreams.

Suddenly she started and raised her eyes. She thought that the man in the frock-coat announcing the programme had called her name. 'Did you call me, Nils?'

Dagni asked her uncle, glancing at him and at once frowned.

Uncle Nils looked at Dagni, either in terror or in rapture. And Aunt Magda, pressing her handkerchief to her mouth, looked at her in the same way.

'What's the matter?' asked Dagni.

Magda clasped her by the hand and whispered: 'Listen!'

Then Dagni heard the man in the frock-coat saying: 'The people in the back rows have asked me to repeat what I said. So, now the celebrated musical composition of Edward Grieg will be played. It is dedicated to the daughter of the woodcutter, Hagerup Pedersen, Dagni Pedersen, on the occasion of her eighteenth birthday.'

Dagni gasped so deeply that her chest hurt. She wanted to suppress with that gasp the tears that flooded into her throat. But it did not help. Dagni bent over and covered her face with her palms.

At first, she heard nothing. A storm erupted inside her. And finally she heard how the shepherd's horn sang out in the early morning, and in response to it, with a hundred voices, a little startled, the string orchestra came towards it.

The melody grew, rising, raging like the wind, took itself up to the treetops, broke off the leaves, ruffled the grass, crashed into the face with cold splashes. Dagni felt the blast of the air emanating from the music and made herself calm. Yes, it was her forest, her birthplace! Her mountains, the songs of the horns, the sound of the sea!

Glass boats made the water foam, the wind trumpeted in their tackle. The sound developed into a chime of forest belfries, to the whistling of the birds turning somersaults in the air, to the halooing of children, to the song of the absent maiden – her sweetheart threw a handful of sand into her window at dawn. Dagni had heard that song at her place in the hills.

So it was him after all! That grey-haired man who had helped her carry home the basket of fir-cones. It was Edward Grieg, the magician and the great musician! She had reproached him for not being able to work quickly enough! And here was the present he had promised to make for her in ten years' time!

Without hiding them, Dagni was crying tears of gratitude. By that time, the music had filled all the space between the earth and the clouds which were hanging over the city. The melodic waves made a light ripple appear on the clouds. The stars were shining through it. The music no longer sang; it was calling her. It was calling her to that land where no sorrows can make love cold, where no one takes away the happiness of another, where the sun shines warmly like a crown on the hair of the good witch in a fairytale.

Suddenly from the flood of sounds a familiar voice arose: 'You are happiness,' it said. 'You are the lustre of the dawn!'

The music fell silent. At first, the applause began slowly; then it burst forth like an eruption.

Dagni got up and quickly went to the park exit. They were all staring at her. Perhaps some of the audience had got the idea in their heads that this girl was the Dagni Pedersen to whom Grieg had dedicated this immortal piece.

'He's dead,' thought Dagni. 'Why? If only it had been possible to see him! If only he could appear here!'

With her heart impetuously beating, she would have run forward to greet him. How she would have clasped him around the neck, pressing her cheeks wet with tears to his, and would have said just one word: 'Thank you!' 'For what?' he would have asked. 'I don't know . . .' Dagni would have said. 'For not forgetting me; for your generosity; for revealing to me that wonderful thing by which people should live.'

Dagni walked around the empty streets. She did not

even notice that Nils, who had been sent by Magda, was following her, trying not to catch her attention. He staggered like a drunk, muttering something about a miracle which had happened to him in his humdrum life.

Dusk still lay over the city, but in the windows the northern dawn could already be seen with its weak gilding.

Dagni went towards the sea. It was resting in a deep slumber without as much as a splash. She clasped her hands together and moaned at the feeling which was still unclear to her, but which was enveloping the whole of her being – the feeling she had for the beauty of this world.

'Hear me, Life!' said Dagni softly. 'I love you.'

And she laughed as she gazed with wide-open eyes at the lights of the steamers, bobbing gently in the transparent grey water.

Nils, who was standing a little way away, heard her laughter and walked home. Now he was sure of Dagni. Now he knew that her life would not be spent in vain.

1954

Notes to text of translation

1   *Kakhetian*: the name of a brand of Armenian wine.

2   *Zamoskvorechye*: the Moscow suburbs on the side of the Moscow River, facing the Kremlin.

3   *dacha*: a house in the country, often privately owned.

4   *'My soul is constrained....'*: words from Pushkin's poem 'Autumn' *(Oysen)*.

5   *Katyusha Maslova*: a character in Tolstoy's novel *Resurrection The Road to Calvary*: a novel by the Soviet writer Aleksei Tolstoy (1883-1945).

6   *Nightingales, nightingales...* part of a well-known World War II song.

7   *I do not like your irony*: words from a poem by N.A. Nekrasov (1821-1877).

8   *M. Voloshin*: a Soviet Russian poet (1877-1932).

9   *The impossible becomes possible....* lines from Aleksandr Blok's poem *Rossiya*.

10   *Let's sit down before taking the road*: Before beginning a journey, it is customary for Russians to sit down and observe silence for a few moments. The action is believed to ensure good fortune.

11   *Saltykov–Shchedrin*: a Russian philosophical writer (1826-1889), whose ideas greatly influenced early 20th century thinkers.

12   *Bread and salt*: proverbial for a basic diet. When guests come to the house, bread and salt are offered as a symbolic greeting.

13   *Maria Pavlovna Chekova*: Chekhov's sister, died in Yalta 1957.

14   *Masha*: here refers to the character in Chekhov's play, *Three Sisters*.

15   *N. Yazykov*: a contemporary of Pushkin (1803-1898).

16   *Christiania* : the name of Oslo until 1925.